Also by Carolee Dean

Take Me There

forget

forget me not

CAROLEE DEAN

Simon Pulse

New York   London   Toronto   Sydney   New Delhi

∧∧∧

SIMON PULSE

An imprint of Simon & Schuster Children's Publishing Division

1230 Avenue of the Americas, New York, NY 10020

First Simon Pulse hardcover edition October 2012

Copyright © 2012 by Carolee Dean

For information about special discounts for bulk purchases, please contact
Simon & Schuster Special Sales at 1-866-506-1949 or business@simonandschuster.com.

The Simon & Schuster Speakers Bureau can bring authors to your live event.

For more information or to book an event contact the Simon & Schuster Speakers

Bureau at 1-866-248-3049 or visit our website at www.simonspeakers.com.

Designed by Mike Rosamilia

The text of this book was set in Adobe Garamond Pro.

Manufactured in the United States of America

2 4 6 8 10 9 7 5 3 1

Library of Congress Cataloging-in-Publication Data

Dean, Carolee. Forget me not / Carolee Dean. p. cm.

Summary: Told from separate viewpoints, Ally discovers that she may have tried to kill
herself, and Elijah, recalling his own suicide attempt, tries to give Ally a reason to live
and escape from the spirits that haunt their high school.

[1. Novels in verse. 2. Interpersonal relations—Fiction. 3. Emotional problems—Fiction.

4. Dead—Fiction. 5. High schools—Fiction. 6. Schools—Fiction. 7. Popularity—

Fiction. 8. Haunted places—Fiction.] I. Title. PZ7.5.D43For 2012

[Fic]—dc23 2011025818

ISBN 978-1-4424-3254-3   ISBN 978-1-4424-3256-7 (eBook)

For Kurt, wherever you may be.
I hope they have stories there.

PART ONE

THE
HA__WAY

Ally

I CAME TO THE HALLWAY

because
I wanted to live.
Deliberately.

No, wait.
That was Thoreau.

I came to the hallway
alone,
while the dew
was still on the roses.

Forget that.
I never liked old hymns.
Besides, it's almost winter
and the roses are
gone
like Thoreau.

I came in peace.
Then I came
to pieces.

Don't bullshit yourself, Ally.
You came to the hallway
because you didn't
have anywhere
else to go.

THE SECOND FLOOR OF HUMANITIES

I sit
on the tiled bench seat
that extends
almost the entire length
of the wall,
looking like
two steps
to nowhere.

They built it
that way because
they were afraid
of what would happen
to real furniture.

Too easy
to abuse
and destroy.

Things that are
breakable
(like me)
don't belong
in high school.

FROM THIS LOCATION

I can see all the way
across the quad,
where a dozen or more kids
sit on a similar tiled bench
waiting for the first bell and
texting like mad,
sending photos
to the dozen or so kids
sitting on a similar tiled bench
in Sci-Tech
waiting for the first bell and
texting like mad,
sending photos (of me?)
to the dozen or so kids
sitting on a similar tiled bench
in the gym
waiting for the first bell and
texting like mad,
sending photos—
they must be of me—
to the thousands
of kids scattered all across
Raven Valley High School.
Texting like mad,
sending photos of ME
EVERYWHERE.

Except to the second floor
of Humanities . . .
because it's a
dead zone.

Another reason
I came to the hallway.

I KNOW

who took the picture,
Davis's sister Brianna,
my former best friend.

She didn't send it out at first.
Didn't send it for nearly two months.
I thought she'd forgotten about it.
Guess I was wrong.

Brianna was standing
in the bathroom
that connects
her room to her brother's.

"Sorry, guys," she said, as the
flash from her cell phone cam
burned the sleep from my eyes.
"I had to document this
moment, because tomorrow
I'm gonna think it was
a friggin' hallucination."
Her face was full of betrayal and
accusation. I had to look away.
I hadn't meant to stay
with him all night. Never meant
for her to know. Intended to go
before first light, but couldn't bring myself
to push his arm away. To slip out
from under the warmth of his embrace.

"Wait, Brianna!" I said as
she turned to leave. "I can explain."

But she just walked away,
and it was a good thing,
because I didn't really have
a single thing to say
in my defense.

HOW IT HAPPENED

It was our first time.
I had come to spend the night
with her and ended up
spending it with him.

I hadn't
planned it
that way.

Bri was asleep and
I'd been staring at the
foreign movie posters on her wall,
thinking about the huge scene Darla
had made when she broke up with Davis
the night before, calling him a liar and cheat
just because he'd loaned some girl in precalc
his math book.

I was thinking about how
he was in the very next room,
alone and available.

I went to the bathroom for a drink of water,
and when I finished filling the glass,
I felt him behind me,
his hot breath on my neck,
his hand on my back.
His fingertips trailing my spine.

In the mirror I saw
him turn and walk
back into his room and
I followed.

At that moment,
Davis Connor
was all
I wanted.

WHEN HE SAW BRIANNA

Davis ran to her door. She
slammed it in his face. *Damn,*
he yelled, turning red with rage,
banging on the wood with his fist.

WARNING

and threatening, but Brianna had
locked herself in her room. He
sat on the bed, trembling.
Darla can't find out. She's

VERY

unpredictable. "I thought she broke up
with you." He showed me his phone.
SORRY ABOUT LAST NIGHT. I'LL
MAKE IT UP TO YOU. *She's more*

FRAGILE

than people realize, he said. *I want
to end it, but she has to think it's
her idea or she'll make my life
a living hell. You won't tell,*

WILL

you? "Of course not," I said.
I was the one who was fragile,
though I didn't know at the time
just how easy it would be for me to

SHATTER.

I SQUEEZED HIS HAND

in reassurance
and said,
"She'll *never* know."

Darla is captain
of the dance team and I
had to see her every afternoon
at practice, but I am
an expert at keeping
my feelings
hidden inside.

"That's what a good actress does,"
my mother used to say

before she left.

"Keep them guessing. Don't
ever let them know
what you're really thinking."

Davis smiled and his eyes
were filled with such relief
that I felt proud.
Yes, I admit it,
proud.

Like I'd done a good deed.

He kissed me
in gratitude
and his lips
took me in.

"This has to stay
our secret," he said,
with a promise in his voice
that if I could stay quiet,
I could be with him again.

My heart rose and fell,
danced and crashed.

I wanted so desperately to walk
down the hallway at school
arm in arm with him,
watching all the other
girls cringe in envy.

I didn't want to be some secret,
tucked away in the back of his bedroom.

"I won't say a word," I said.

A little bird tried to warn me.
It was whispering words like
Liar . . . and . . . Cheat . . .
but I couldn't hear what
it was saying.

At that moment my
heart was beating
too loudly to
hear anything else.

I LOOK ACROSS THE COURTYARD AT THE FAB

There is yellow crime

   scene tape at the bottom

      of the stairs to the Fine Arts

         Building, in front of the entrance

            to Brady Theater. I wonder if the

               forensics class has created

                  another mock murder or if

                     the crime is real. At this

                        school it could go either way.

POLICE LINE DO NOT CROSS POLICE LINE DO NOT CROSS POLICE

HAUNTED HALLWAY

Second period.
Kids start buzzing
down the F Hall in
the center of the school,
turning left onto the
G Hall at the front
of the building, and
making their way
outside like wasps
suddenly freed
from a nest.

The hum
is deafening.
They aren't really free.
They have five minutes
to make it outside
to another brick building,
another pointless class,
another hour of futility.

Not one of them
goes through the door
that leads to the H Hall,
where I sit.
They hurry past it
but they
never enter.

That's because there
aren't any classes
on the H Hall. The
rooms are all used
for storage.

Besides, there's
no way out
of the H Hall except for
a handicapped elevator
at the far end, and you have
to have a special key for that.

But I've known kids with
broken legs who would go
all the way to the other side
of the building to use that
elevator, rather than walk
through the H Hall.

There's a very good
reason for this.

The H Hall is haunted.

I used to walk
all the way
around the building
to avoid it, but I don't
mind it anymore.

I have ghosts of my own.

THE GHOSTS OF RAVEN VALLEY HIGH

A hundred years ago the school was a convent.
Then after a scandal involving a young nun and a
Jesuit priest, the convent was sold and Our
Sisters of Divine Charity became the House of

Fallen Angels

and eventually a military institute. Unfortunately, there
was a tragic incident involving a young private and a
girl from a nearby prep school and it closed down. It's
hard to follow the rule of no guns in school when you're

preparing for war.

It was later reopened as a small private university, which
is the reason the buildings have names like Sci-Tech.
Then the head of the English Department made off
with a bunch of money tucked inside a book of stolen

metaphors.

The property sat vacant for ten years and became a home
to migrating birds and vagrants. Eventually the city auctioned
off the land and the buildings. The school board bought it
cheap, thinking it would be the perfect location

for a high school.

OUT THE WINDOW

I see Brianna

walking across the grass
down on the quad
and my first impulse is to wave.

She looks upset,
and that worries me.
But then I remember
she's not my friend anymore.

So why do I still care?

I think about how her
Saturday Night Live
imitations used to make
me laugh so hard I cried.

I think about late-night
brownie binges, Halloween
costume shopping sprees,
and Popsicle brain freezes.

But then I remember
how when she became a vegan,
I was supposed to become one too.
And when she boycotted Walmart,
she gave me a two-hour lecture
when I bought a bottle of suntan lotion
from "the corporate oppressors."

I was worried in middle school
when I started getting all the lead roles
in the school plays, but then she decided
she'd rather be a director, which
ended up being the perfect job
for a control freak.

She's just like my dad,
always trying to get people to fit
into nice straight lines.

I hate control freaks.

But when I see
her Girl Power backpack,
her yin-yang tattoo,
and her blond dreds,
my very first impulse

is to smile and wave.

WRITE IT OUT

That's what Ms. Lane,
my writing teacher,
would say.
Spill it out onto
the page.
Sometimes it's
the only way

for thoughts heavy
as bricks
to become feathers
and fly away.

I could go
to her class.
Get my head
together.

I'd sit next to
Elijah.

I wonder if
he's heard.

Even if he has,
I know

he
wouldn't say
a word.

ELIJAH WEARS BLACK

leather biker pants even
though he doesn't ride

a bike. Total geek. Loose white
shirt and leather boots make him

look like Orlando
from *As You Like It*. He went
to the psych ward last

spring when his brother, Frank, died.
When he came back he kept to

himself. Sat alone
during lunch scribbling in his
notebook and then he

spent a whole month speaking in
iambic pentameter.

He knows what it's like
to be the campus joke. I
would be safe with him.

The other kids think he's lost
his mind. I think he's found it.

Shakespeare is a mask
to hide the pain. I wonder—
if I found a mask,

put it on, and tied it fast,
would I be okay again?

I HAVE A MOLESKINE NOTEBOOK

I keep in the back
pocket of my jeans.

It's just like the one
Hemingway used to write in,
before he blew out his brains.

It's filled with poems
and letters to Ernest.

I began writing to him
in September,
when everything started
with Davis.
Ernest was dead,
so I knew
he could keep a secret.

Maybe if I tell him what happened,
he'll help me figure out what to do.

I don't even know where to start,
but I open the notebook anyway,
because I don't have anywhere to go,
and I know, it's gonna be
                    a long,
                        long day.

PART TWO

T _ _ _
MANY
QUESTI_NS

Elijah

INTERROGATION

They're calling all the freshmen
into Admin (aka Watchdog Tower).

It got its name from
the winged wolves
perched on the four corners
of what used to be a church.

We go into the conference room,
one by one, so they can question us
about what happened to Ally.

Officer Richie,
the campus cop,
and some guy in a suit.
It's the suit who does all the talking.

"How long have you known Ally Cassell?"

It's the middle of October,
but the room
is hot as Hades. I wonder
if they turned up the heat on purpose.
To make us all sweat.

"Since elementary school,"
I tell the man.

He makes a note on his legal pad.
"How did you meet her?"
I can't imagine how this is relevant,
but I don't want to seem difficult.
It's easy to get a reputation
for being difficult.

Once you do,
they never stop
watching you.

"I was in *A Christmas Carol* with her
and Brianna Connor in the third grade.
Ally was the Ghost of Christmas Past.
Bri was the Ghost of Christmas Future,
and I was the Ghost of Christmas Present."

"I see," he says, looking me up and down
as if he's already made up his mind that I'm
trouble, just because my hair is in a ponytail
and my ears and nose are pierced.
But my comment seems
to have great significance
because he takes copious notes.

Then he peers at me
over his black-rimmed glasses.
"Would you say you were *close*?"

We were in every school play together
from third grade to seventh.
Then my brother died
the summer before eighth
and I sort of went AWOL,
but this is none of the man's business,
so I don't say anything.

I remember you, Ally,
out beneath the stars that night
at the party at the end of middle school,
when I finally started coming back around.
Your hair was the color of gold shining in the moonlight.
Your chin turned up to the stars under
the soft glow of the streetlight.
I should have called you afterward,
but I was too afraid.
I'm so sorry.
Maybe things would have
turned out differently if I had.

"I asked if you were close?"

"Off and on."

"When was the last time you saw Ms. Cassell?"

"In sixth period, yesterday afternoon," I say.

Ally, remember when I told you
I was taking a creative writing class?
I said I was tired of reading lines
written by someone else.
It felt like my whole life
had been scripted and
directed by strangers.
I said you should sign up too.
But I didn't really think you would.

When I saw you in class that first day,
I told myself high school was gonna be
a brand-new start.
I wanted so badly to believe
you were there because you had a crush on me,
like the one I had on you,
but then you joined the dance team and
started running with the popular crowd.
Then the rumors started circulating
about you and Davis.
That picture told the rest of the story.

"What was her mood yesterday afternoon?"

You were hiding under your hoodie,
but I could still see that you'd dyed your hair
jet-black, as if that would fool anyone.

You were writing on your arm
with a permanent marker the words,

I HATE MY LIFE. I HATE MY LIFE. I HATE MY LIFE.

I asked if you were okay, and you started to cry.
You seemed so small then. I wanted to hold you.

You are small.
Barely five foot three,
but you have a way
of filling a room
that makes you seem
bigger than life.

Like the day you stood up in class,
did a 2Pac impression,
sang a rap you'd made up,
and had us all cheering.

You nearly had us convinced,
you were a dead black rapper,
but then you always were
a special kind of actor.

I guess that's because
you didn't just crave the limelight;
you needed it.

Some kids complained that you always had to be
the center of attention.
But I knew the truth. You were just looking
for something to fill up the big, black hole
inside your soul. Like I was.

Yesterday, when I saw you shrinking
into your coat, it broke my heart.
Just before the bell rang, you turned to me and said,
"Would you like to have my picture?"
There was desperation in your eyes.
I didn't know how to reply, so I nodded.

You reached
into your pocket,
pulled out your school ID,
and set it on my desk.

Then you disappeared down the crowded hall.
I tried to follow you.
I even went to your next class,
but you never showed.

The man in the suit
clears his throat,
a world away,
as he waits for my answer.
I can barely remember the question.

"I asked about her mood," he says.

"She seemed a little depressed."

"Why?"

I'm sure he already knows.
He's spent all morning interrogating
your so-called friends.
"Somebody sent a naked picture of her around the school?"

"Was it you?"

"No!" I say, and my voice sounds too big
and the room seems too small.

"You *claim* that the last time you saw her was in your writing
class."

"That's what I told you."

Why are they questioning me like this
when it's obvious what happened to you?
But the students are upset
and parents are in an uproar.
They want answers
and solutions
and guarantees

that what happened to you
won't happen to their kids.

"Are you sure you weren't on the roof
of Brady Theater with her last night?"

"No." My palms are sweating. Does he see?
Why are my palms sweating?

"What if I told you that someone saw you
going up there with her?"
He has to be making this up,
but my entire body starts to tremble.

"I'd say they're lying."

He opens up a briefcase and pulls out a file
with my name on it.

"Do you ever have problems with your memory?"

Are the walls moving?
I could swear they're closing in.

"No."

"But you did spend some time in a psychiatric hospital
last spring."

It's not exactly a question,
but I answer it anyway.
"Four weeks."

"May I ask why?"

"You may ask, but that doesn't mean I'll answer."
Why torture me? I'm sure it's all in the file.

He leans toward me and his face becomes
hard as stone.

"We know someone was up on the roof
with Allison Cassell
at one a.m. this morning.
There's an image on the surveillance camera.
It looks an awful lot like you. Can you prove it wasn't?"

There's no surveillance camera up there,
or else the school would have found out months ago
about all the partying that happens on the roof, and
they would have put a swift end to that, I'm sure.
Maybe that's why they're harassing students.
They've been up there and seen
the empty bottles and makeshift bongs.
If it ends up in the newspaper,
the school officials will need an explanation.

But he's fishing. Probably told the same story to every kid
he's talked to, just waiting to see if someone will crack
and tell him you tumbled in a drunken daze.
No nasty attempt to end your life.
Nobody pushed you
over the edge.

So why is my heart beating so damn fast?

I was home
feeling sorry for myself,
writing letters to my dead brother
and wondering why you fell for Davis
and not for me.
Forgive me, Ally. I should have
been there for you. I knew you were in trouble.
I *should* have been up there on the roof.

"Have you ever used drugs?" he asks me.

The room is on fire. I've got to get out of here. I stand.

"Sit down, Mr. McCoy," says the man in the suit.

I don't know how, but from somewhere,
I find the strength to say,
"Do I need a lawyer?"

"Why would you think that?"

If I stay here one moment longer,
I'm gonna be in deep shit.
I take a step toward the door.

"Sit down, Elijah," says Officer Richie.

"Am I under arrest?"

"No."

"Then you can't keep me here."

I don't know if this is true or not.
I know people out in the real world have rights,
but this isn't the real world.
This is high school.

I take another step toward the door.

"Sit down!" says the man in the suit,
but he makes no move to stop me,
so I open the door
and I run.

OLD MAN WINTERS

stands in the middle of the hallway,
right in front of the principal's office,
mopping the same spot over
and over and over again.
He never
     changes location
and he always
     wants to talk to me
          just because one day I made the mistake
               of saying hello. Nobody else ever talks to him.
                    There's a good reason for this. Nobody else sees him.

"Now where are you going
in such an all-fire hurry?" he asks.

I don't reply and this just makes him
more persistent. He raises his voice
as I pass. "Slow down, sonny,
you don't wanna slip and break your neck.
Why don't you stop and have a cookie? The
missus bakes 'em up fresh every Monday."
He pulls something petrified from his pocket.
It's a different item every time.
Today it's a dead mouse.

I try not to glance in his direction.
I just look straight ahead
and keep on running.

MR. TOOMS OFFICE

I'm racing down the hall
of the administration building
when I hear another voice yell, "Elijah!"

I turn around and see my counselor,
Mr. Tooms, standing outside
the door of his office.
Someone who's alive and real.

Someone I can trust
with a few things, anyway.

He motions me inside
to safety.

I go in and collapse
on the threadbare couch
and I can't help it.
I start to cry.

HE JUST LETS ME SIT THERE

blubbering like a baby
until there's nothing left.
When I finally look up, I see
the same gray walls I've stared at
week after week for the past three months.
When I started at Raven Valley High, his office
was the first place I visited.

Mr. Tooms has done his best
to brighten up the space
with inspirational posters
and *Doonesbury* comic strips.

He has a bookcase filled with knickknacks
and an entire shelf dedicated
to his stuffed-bird collection.
There's a parrot dressed like a doctor
and another one dressed like a biker,
complete with a Harley and a bandanna,
and a black bird lying on a couch
that he says is his Jungian dark side.
I don't know what that means,
but that one is a real conversation starter.
At the top of the shelf is a clay jar with the words
ASHES OF OBNOXIOUS TEENAGERS.

"Bad morning?" he asks.

"Yeah. You could say that."

I've been interrogated by the police
and accosted by a dead janitor,
but I don't dare mention number two.
Even sympathetic counselors have a limit
to what they will believe.

"Wanna beat up Barney?"
He hands me a foam baton
and points to an inflated purple dinosaur
in the corner of the room.

I put the baton on the couch. "I don't think it would help."

"Are you going to be okay?"

What he's really asking is whether or not
he needs to fill out a risk assessment. He's
hoping I'm not gonna go off the deep end,
like I did after Frankie died.

I let my hair grow out and wouldn't eat.
Pierced my nose. Starting piecing shoes
together out of parts of army boots.
And then one night I took a bunch of pills.
That's when I started seeing dead people.

"I'm okay," I lie.

"Do you want to talk about what happened to Ally?"

I feel sick all over again, like someone turned me
inside out and stepped on my guts.

"I want to hurt the people who hurt her,"
I blurt out before I realize this might sound like
some sort of threat that he will have to document in my file.

I wait for a reaction.

He nods and says, "I understand why you'd feel that way."

Who am I kidding? I don't have
a malicious bone in my body.
I stand. "I gotta get back to class."

"Elijah," he says as I turn to leave.

"Yes."

"The next few days are going to be rough.
Come back anytime you want to."

"I will," I tell him.

Then I walk out into the hall
and I come face-to-face with
Brianna Connor.

BRIANNA'S EYES

are swollen and red. She's been crying.
"I didn't do it," she says, shaking her head violently
so the dreds fly back and forth.
"Everybody is saying it's me, but I didn't do it."

She sounds sincere, but then, she's a good actor.
Almost as good as me.
Not nearly as good as Ally.

The old Bri never would have texted pictures
of her best friend all over the school,
but we've all changed since the days
when we hung out by the pool,
rehearsing lines, playing charades,
roasting hot dogs on the grill.

I had a meltdown and had to go away.
Bri became an activist for any cause she could find,
preaching about the evils of red meat and fossil fuels.

Ally rose
then fell
from the ladder of popularity
before she'd made it halfway through
her freshman year.

"I didn't send the picture," Bri says convincingly.

Maybe not, but then who? And where the hell were you
when your best friend needed you? I want to say.
But I don't, because . . .

I'm guilty, too.

I wasn't there for Ally either.
Nobody was.

I CONVINCED MYSELF

that Ally was better off without me.
That Bri was better off without me,
because I was a nut job.

What did I have to offer anyone,
especially a girl like Ally?

Now I realize too late
that she was on shakier ground than I was.

I look at Brianna's frantic expression
and wonder if she's becoming
a nut job too.

Maybe everybody has
the potential.

THE BELL RINGS

and it's time for history.
I walk toward Humanities, take
the stairs up to the second floor, go inside, and stop
at the door to the H Hall. I can't go
there yet. That's gonna take some nerve.

My heartbeat sprints, I break out in a sweat.
The air is cold as ice. My breath comes fast.
I step away and walk on to my class.

I once spent three days sitting on that hall.
It's the perfect place to disappear.
But if you stay too long, then there's a good
chance you'll never make it out of there.

I know that's where you've gone.
I want to tell you that you need to run,
but would you believe me if I tried?

You used to be so confident, so cool.
In middle school you never gave a crap
what the other kids said about you.

I didn't know that there was something deep
inside of you that made you want to be
part of the crowd you always used to mock.
I think you lost yourself when you became
someone who had to watch her clothes, her walk,
her weight. It was a losing game.

And then the very crowd you counted on,
turned on you, so you tried to take your life.

I kissed you once. I wonder if you think
about that night we all played Truth or Dare
at that party at the end of eighth
grade, when you still didn't seem to care
what people thought of you or what they said.

You asked me for the truth about that night
they took me to the psych ward, and I said,
"I tried to die but didn't do it right."
You didn't turn away or treat me like
you were scandalized or even scared.
You just smiled and said, "I'm glad you're back."
Then it was my turn and so I dared
you to go out with me for a walk.
All I really wanted was to talk.

When we were out beneath the stars I said,
"Milady, would you like to try a dance?"
You smiled and then we two-stepped in the yard.
I finally got the nerve to hold your hand,
hardly believing we were there alone
and that you didn't try to pull away.
You asked me why I'd taken on a tone
that made me sound like I was from a play.

It seemed to me that only words and rhymes
made any sense. Only they were safe.
Nouns and verbs constructed in straight lines
made the world a saner, safer place.

You laughed at me but I didn't complain.
You stepped in close and I could feel your heart.
I wrapped you in my arms and pressed my lips.
You opened up your mouth and let me in.

It seemed we stayed out there for hours and days.
I wove a bracelet of forget-me-nots.
Tied it on your wrist.
We kissed again.
It was the first time that I ever made
out. You said good-bye and walked away.
I should have called, but I was too afraid.

Whatever happens, Ally, please know this—
you'll always be my first love. My first kiss.

PART THREE

A BR_EF H_STORY OF MY L_FE

Ally

SAY CHEESE

Just get your pencil moving,
Ms. Lane always says,
so I take out my pencil and write
the only thing that comes to my mind.

My first word was "cheese."

My earliest memory is of my mother
taking my picture at the park.
"Smile and say cheese," she told me,
as I sat in the swing,
wondering why it wasn't moving.

"Smile and say cheese," she told me, as I sat
in front of a sandcastle she had built, because
she didn't want me to get my new sundress dirty.

I was a late bloomer.
I hadn't said mama or dada or baba,
googoo or nana or gaga.

But she didn't take me to a doctor.
Instead she took me to a talent scout
who was looking for a baby for an
organic carrot commercial.

"Smile and say cheese," my mother said,
as the man adjusted the camera lens.
Then the bright lights flashed in my eyes,
something went *click* in my brain,
and I spoke my first word . . .

"Cheese."

A CHRISTMAS CAROL

Mom took me
to try out
for *A Christmas Carol*
in third grade.

That's where
I met Bri and Elijah.

I got a part
in every school play
after that.

I never really felt alive
unless I was up onstage.

It's like that old saying,
"If a tree falls in the forest,
and no one hears it,
does it make a sound?"

If I'm here
but nobody sees me,

am I really alive?

THE FAIREST

In fifth grade I got the part of
Snow White in the spring play,
but Dad convinced me
to let Bri have it because I'd already
played Sleeping Beauty in the fall.
"You don't always have to be the star," he said.

When my mother found out, she hit the roof.
"Never, never give up what is rightfully yours,"
she told me. "Don't be afraid to shine.
Your true friends will be your biggest fans.
And remember this above all else . . .

Only one can be the fairest."

Something inside of me
broke loose then.
I wasn't afraid anymore
of being better than everyone else,
and I became unstoppable.
It was as if until that moment
I'd been trying to keep the
sun from rising.

Dad never understood.

He warned me, saying,
"Shooting stars sometimes crash and burn."

Leave it to Dad to try to hold me down,
like he tried to do with my mother,
until she got away.

I INHERITED MY LOVE OF THE STAGE

from Mom.
She used to spend
nearly every night
at the community theater
rehearsing or performing
or taking acting classes.

My parents fought about
it all the time. Dad said
she should be home
taking care of her family.

Mom said we should move
to California or New York,
where she could get real acting jobs,
and that a man who sold
pharmaceutical supplies for a living
could do that anywhere.

For years she begged and pleaded,
and then one day,
right after I turned twelve,
she just gave up
and left.

I begged her to take me with her,
but my father wouldn't let her.
She said she'd get a lawyer
and fight for custody,
but she didn't have much money.

The acting jobs
were few and far between,
like her letters.
Until one day they just
                      stopped
                              coming.

I know my father is hiding them,
though he won't admit it.

And for that I hate him.

THERE'S SOMETHING DARK

in the corner
of the hallway,
but every time
I try to look,
it disappears.

There's something
cold in the corner
of the hallway,
but every time
I go to check it out,
it moves away.

There's something talking to me
from the corner of the hallway.
I can't see what it is,
but I lean in close to listen.

I used to hear voices
in the halls,
whispering things like
slut,   liar,   whore

I hear voices
on the H Hall, too,
even though there's
nobody here but me.

They're telling me this
is the only place where

Nobody can touch me.
Nobody can hurt me.
Nobody can reach me.

"You can stay here forever," they whisper.

SOME KIDS SAY

Some kids say that, about ten years ago,
a senior tripping out on ecstasy
hung himself from the rafters on the H Hall.
There used to be rafters, but

some kids say that after the incident,
the school board put up ceiling tiles
so you couldn't see where he did it.
That's also when they closed the hall
off with a big steel door and started
using the classrooms for storage.

Some kids say that at night
they see a dim light moving
back and forth across the hall
when the building is supposed to be empty.

Some kids say that in the middle
of the hallway the air is ice-cold,
and if you happen to be alone,
you can hear voices whispering to you,
telling you to do terrible things.
They seem to come from inside
your head, and one kid put his skull
through the glass trying to get the voices to stop.

Some kids say that if the tardy bell rings,
the steel door locks, and you can't get off the
hallway until the next class period, but by
that time you will have lost your mind,
and no matter where they take you from there,
you'll always think you're on the hallway.

Some kids say that all the stories are a bunch of crap
that the teachers made up because they want to keep
kids off the H Hall. It's the shortest route between
the copy room on the second floor and the teachers'
lounge on the first floor.

Some kids say I'm a slut because I slept with Davis
when he was still going with Darla. They don't know
what she's like. They don't know how long he tried to
break it off with her so he could be with me.

I'm glad I can't hear
what some kids are saying.

AFTER THE TARDY

bell the courtyard clears out and
when it gets quiet

a black raven lands on the
railing outside my window.

Funny how I am
already thinking of the
hallway as my own.

The bird flaps his wings and caws.
The pigeons above cower.

I don't remember
if ravens are predators.
Should have been paying

more attention in science
class but too late for that now.

I'm getting a big,
fat F. My father will freak.
But it was hard to

keep my mind on school work when
my phone was flashing hate texts.

Teens have their own set
of acronyms. BFF.
But not anymore.

LOL. Who's laughing now?
WTF is more

like it. I check the
screen before I remember
that I'm in a no

service zone. That's good. My cell
used to be my lifeline, but

now it feels like a
BSOD. A Blue Screen
of Death. When your whole

life has been wiped off the hard
drive and no one knows you're gone.

MISSING DAVIS

I miss you, Davis.

I miss
the way
you would trace
your fingers across
my face and tell me
I was beautiful.

I miss
the way you looked
at me when we were together,
like I was the only person in the world.

I miss
how when I was with you,
you made me feel smart
and funny and important.

I miss
the girl I became
every time you entered the room.

I miss
the text messages
you would send me when I knew
you were with her, saying
how you couldn't wait until Friday night.

I miss
the feeling of white heat filling my body
when I read what you wanted to do
to me the next time we were alone.

I even miss
almost getting caught and hurrying
to delete your messages before
my dad could read them.

But most of all I miss
how sometimes, when I least expected
it, you would send me a message that said

"I miss you, Ally."

IT WAS THE WEEK MY MOTHER LEFT

That's when I started noticing
Brianna's older brother.
Up until then he'd just been
the annoying creep who
kicked us out of the game room
every time his friends came over.

The fall of our sixth-grade year,
Bri's house became a jock hangout.
Davis was the only freshman
to make the varsity football team.
At fifteen, he was the first-string quarterback
for the Raven Valley Raptors.

There was an endless parade
of girls through the halls, licking
their lips and competing
with each other for a look.

One night
Brianna took her brother's
cell phone while he was
passed out in the den.

We had a big laugh
as we looked through
the thirty pictures of
girls who'd sent photos
of themselves
in bras and thongs and less.

I laughed along,
but secretly I wondered
what it would take
for Davis to notice me.

FRESHMAN FALL

Davis barely knew that I existed
till I got to RVHS, his domain.

He's a senior. He'll be leaving soon
for college. Desperation made me bold.

Brianna was organizing shoes.
I told her I was going for a swim.

A hot September night, I slipped into
a two-piece barely covering the breasts

that popped up unexpectedly in June.
I think that's what he must have noticed first.

Does that make him a pervert or does it
make me a perv because I was praying

that he would notice something? He was walking
through the backyard when he saw the Twins.

Mary-Kate and Ashley they were called
by all the boys. I didn't have a clue

that after only two short weeks of school,
my body parts had nicknames. He sat down

on the lounge chair next to mine and looked
at both the Twins, then recognized my face.

Blushed crimson red, looked in my eyes, and said,
"Ally Cassell, when did you grow up?"

I should have been offended that it took
him all those years to say seven words to me.

But I was too busy relishing the sound
of my name on his lips and in his mouth.

IT'S IRONIC

but I think Davis noticed me
partly because of Darla.

She invited all the freshman Ravenettes
over to her
house for makeovers.

"We have an image to maintain,"
she and her friends told us
as they showed us how to wax
and pluck and blend.

My mother left before she had a chance
to teach me about things like that and
Brianna didn't care about hair and makeup.

"You'll be eating lunch with the team
from now on at the jock tables,"
Darla informed us.

She also told us she had three objectives for the year—
   Get the lead in *My Fair Lady*
      Make captain of the dance team
         And hang on to Davis Connor
            long enough for him to take her to prom.

Everyone told her number three
would be the biggest challenge.
Davis never dated a girl
longer than two weeks.
But Darla said she was different.
She knew exactly
what a guy like Davis needed.

DAVIS

Every Friday
I would spend
the night with Brianna,
but as soon as she was asleep
I'd slip into Davis's arms.

She thought the day
she caught me with him
was the only time,
but she was wrong.
It was just the start.
We had to be
more cautious.
There were risks.
Stolen moments
were all
we really had.
But a moment can last
a lifetime, some have said.

His breath was like a
scorching summer wind
across my neck, my back,
my eyes, my throat.
His body moved across mine
as he sent shock waves
through the marrow of my bones.

He'd say, *I love you*, then he'd hold me tight
and tell me that I really was the one
he wanted to be with, but first he had
to break away from Darla.
I held on to that fragile hope
for days, then weeks.

But true to her word,
Darla Johnson always
found a way
to make him stay.

ERNEST HEMINGWAY

You were a writer
but you didn't write a note,
leaving us all to speculate
on why you took your life.

Your father shot himself
and I know that had to
bring you down,
but was it what did you in?

Some say you had a rare disease
that infected your brain.

Did you think about death
in that burning plane?

You lived too fast, you played too hard,
you ran around, you had four wives.

But I know the real reason you took your
life, wrote about loss, and drank too much.

You shot yourself at sixty-one
because of something you lost
when you were young.

It happens to the best of us.

You never
got over
your
first love.

NANA CASSELL

is standing in front of the FAB,
pointing her cane at the school principal,
then at the yellow crime-scene tape,
then back at the principal.

He's trying to tell her something,
but she won't let him get in a word.

I can't figure out,
for the life of me,
what she's doing here at my school.

She came to stay with us when Mom left,
to help take care of me, she told my father.

It was true, I guess, but she also needed
a place to stay after her third stint in rehab.
She loves her vodka. About the only thing
she and Mom have in common.

Dad finally got tired of her and bought her
a one-way ticket to an old-folks home—
in Florida.

So what in the world is she doing here
at my school, yelling at the school principal?

LUNCH WITH THE IN CROWD

The bell rings and kids flood onto the quad for lunch.
Darla Johnson and the other girls from the dance team
sit at a series of picnic benches reserved for the athletes.

When I told Brianna
the first week of school
that I was supposed to eat lunch
with the Ravenettes,
she went ballistic.

"You can't be serious," she said,
her face turning the color of her eggplant sandwich.

"You can come too," I said,
but I knew she'd never go anywhere near her brother
or the other jocks.

"I'll pass," she told me.

She was in a bad mood because
the drama teacher had told her
she didn't need an assistant director
for the play. She tried to talk me
into boycotting the tryouts
and the performance,
but I refused.

Bri grabbed her sack lunch
and started to leave,
but then turned back around.
"By the way,
that eye shadow makes you look
like a hooker."

I was so mad, I couldn't see straight.
But mostly I was glad
that she refused to come with me,
because it's hard to create a new image
when you have old friends
who keep trying to hold you back.

THINGS GOT WEIRD

between Bri and me
after that.

I had dance practice
every afternoon.
Bri starting hanging
with the Goths,

and the only time I saw her
was when I came over
late on Friday to spend the night.

It took her a while
to figure out
that the person
I really came to see
was Davis.

I guess that's when
she decided
to ruin my life.

I SEE ELIJAH

walking across the courtyard,
with Bri following behind him.
He stops and looks up at me
as I stand
in the window.

I step back
into the darkness.

Did he see
me?

Does he know
I'm here?

Does he ever think
about that night at
the end of eighth grade
when we played Truth or Dare?

He was so shy and sweet
and I thought about him
for days afterward,
but he never called.

Then I hooked up
with Davis.

Does Elijah remember
that night,
or did he forget
about it like I forgot
about it

and everything else?

THIRD LUNCH

starts at 12:35.
I see
Elijah.
He carries
a slice of pizza.
Sits at a table
next to Oscar Smith,
who is in a wheelchair.

Oscar uses a small
computer to communicate,
because he can't talk.
He can't press the buttons
too well either, because his hands
are clenched in perpetual fists,
but he has a bright orange pencil
clutched in his hand
that he uses to press the keys.

Elijah is a student aid
in Oscar's special ed class.
I wonder if that's why
he eats with Oscar
or if it's because
Elijah
doesn't have any friends.

I know
how terrible it feels
to walk out
onto the quad
filled with a thousand
other students
and not have a
single person to sit with.

To be friendless
in a crowd
is the worst
kind
of
loneliness.

WILLY J

Will Jones, Davis's best friend,
stays out on the quad
for First Lunch, then Second
Lunch, then Third.

There are certain people
security doesn't mess with.

He walks past a freshman,
grabs the pizza right
out of his hands, and keeps
on walking.

Will devours everything
but the crust in one bite.
He uses the remaining bread
to lure the pigeons.

When one of them gets
close enough, he kicks it
just for fun.
Blood and feathers go flying.

Is that what Darla
is doing to Davis?
Luring him in,
only to destroy him?

Like she did to me.
I shudder when I remember
how I let Will
touch me,
just because I wanted
to make Davis jealous.

It was Darla's idea
to set me up
with him for homecoming.
Too late I realized that
what happened afterward

was all part of her plan.

THE SPARROW AND THE HAWK

Thinking about predators and prey
reminds me of the day
the hawk landed by the hedge
near our front door.

I was heading out to take
a walk, but I stopped
and watched
the strong neck,
russet plumes,
deep brown eyes, and strut
of the predatory bird.

Saw feathers lying
on the ground.
Feared it might be hurt.
Heard rustling.
Saw one eye
of a small
sparrow
as it peered
out from the
shadows.

Now I know
just how it feels
to be the sparrow
in the bush.

SIXTH PERIOD

and security is sweeping the halls.
The men in red T-shirts are out busting

balls. Telling the stragglers to get to their
classes. Making sure wanderers have

signed teacher passes. The bathrooms are
locked so you can't even pee till you

go to the office and ask for a key. If left
unattended, the restroom's the place where

kids go to get stoned, and at least in one case,
a child was conceived in a second-floor stall,

and twice a light fixture was used in a brawl.
There's ranking in, dealing, and tatting. Huffing

of Axe, puking, and cutting. Foul things
happen on the bathroom floor. Crap! A red

shirt's walking up to the door. I look to the
left and I look to the right. Nothing but tile

and no place to hide. So I sit very still, just sit
there and stare. And he walks right on by like

I'm
           not
                   even
                           there.

ONE OF THE SPECIAL ED TEACHERS

Walks onto the H Hall
pushing Oscar Smith,
using the tray
on his wheelchair
to hold the
copies she has made.

I press my body
against the wall, but
Oscar sees me as they
head for the elevator.
No! says the voice
coming out
of his computer.

Does something
from out of the shadows
move toward him,
or is it my imagination?

His arms and legs
begin to flail.
His head jerks
to one side
as if someone
has slapped him
and he groans.
He presses his
orange pencil

into the device
mounted on a metal bar
attached
to his chair.

The words *Get out!*
come screaming
in a voice
that sounds
like it belongs
to a robot.

"What's wrong with you,
Oscar?" the teacher asks.
"Are you hurt?"
The voice just
keeps howling,
rocking the hall
like a lowrider
with the bass
turned up too high.
Get out! Get out! Get out!

The teacher pushes
Oscar
into the elevator,
and the voice stops.

Then the strangest
thing happens.
Just as the
elevator doors
start to close,
Oscar extends his arm,
and his pencil
goes airborne.
It flies between
the doors,
causing them
to stay open
just a crack.

Did he do it on purpose?
I step out into the open
to get a better look at him.

He turns his head,
stares at me,
and there is something
in his eyes
telling me

to run.

The teacher peers
into the H Hall.
"What are you
looking at, Oscar?"

She doesn't see me,
though I'm in plain view.
Then she picks up
the pencil
and the

doors

slide

shut

HIDE AND SEEK

I sit there shuddering
for the longest time,
wondering why that woman
didn't say anything.
It was like I was invisible.

I used to feel invisible all the time.
That's why I loved the stage,
because when I heard people clapping,
I knew they could see me.

Dad said it wasn't healthy
to need to be the center of attention
all the time.
He said I should make some
changes when I got to high school.
He was sure the cure was team sports.

"Sign up for anything,
I don't care, as long as you join a team."

He groaned when I came home with a
permission slip for the Ravenettes,
the dance squad that performs
at all the big games,
especially when he saw how much
money he was going to have to spend
on the outfits.
Eventually he signed it, though.

It was hard work, but I got in great shape.
Guys would
turn their heads to stare at me.
Then Davis noticed me—

He'd look at me and I'd think,
I'm here, I'm alive, I matter.

I liked the attention.
Okay, I loved it!
To be absolutely honest,
I needed it
the way some people
need heroin.

I'M DEFINITELY

not going to English class.
Brianna is there.

Might as well skip PE, too.
And dance team practice is out.

Looks like I will spend
the whole day on the hallway.
Watching other kids,

wondering if their lives are
hopeless and screwed up like mine.

THE FINAL BELL RINGS

I stand to leave, but out on
the balcony I

see Darla Johnson pacing.
Is she waiting there for me?

She walks back and forth,
cocks her head, struts, preens. Looks through
the window. At me?

She's the hawk on the sidewalk.
I'm the sparrow in the bush.

I sit back down and
instantly understand what
it feels like to know

you will soon be plucked apart
and eaten alive. Will she

leave my heart on the
sidewalk with the old, dry gum—
black spot on the quad—

or will she save it for her
dessert? I look at the clock.

My bus will soon be
leaving, but I suddenly
don't want to go home.

My feet are glued to the floor.
I cannot leave the hallway.

DAVIS WALKS OUT

and Darla kisses his cheek.
He smiles and puts
his arm around her waist.

He doesn't look miserable
and unhappy.

She was waiting for him,
not me.

To her I am dead.
To him I am dead.

It doesn't matter.
I've decided.

I'm

never

ever

ever

going to leave

the hallway.

PART FOUR

THE VIEW
FR_M
THE R__F

Elijah

THE FAB

You can get to the roof of the FAB
by way of a fire ladder left from the days
when the building was a dormitory.

Or you can go inside the building,
find the unmarked door by the janitor's closet,
and just walk up to the top. The door is
supposed to be locked, but the knob is old
and rusted and it doesn't take much
to push your way through.

Bri and I opt for number two.
We don't talk about it, we just walk
in silence to the FAB
when we hear the last bell ring.

When we get up on top, I look around
for hidden surveillance cameras. There
aren't any, but I do see smashed beer cans,
a broken bong, and assorted condom wrappers.
I go to the edge and look down
at the yellow tape,
wondering why it's there,
when the real tragedy
happened up here on the roof.

I smell something burning
and turn to see Bri sitting
by a metal box, lighting a cigarette.

"When did you start smoking?"

"What does it matter?"

"Seems like a strange habit for a health nut."

"Just because I don't want to consume
the rotting carcasses of dead animals
doesn't mean I'm a health nut."

As if to emphasize her point, she
picks up a tequila bottle and drinks
the dregs. She tries to look tough,
but her hand is trembling.

"We should have done something,"
I say, looking back at the quad,
where half the kids are scurrying to
buses. The other half don't seem to be
in a hurry to leave. After all, this is where
the social scene is going down.

"What could we have done?"

"I don't know. We should have been there for her."

"I'm not the one who dumped my best friend to become a
Ravenette."

"Were you jealous of her?"

"Not anymore."

She flicks her cigarette away
and joins me at the edge of the roof,
looking down at the yellow tape.

"There isn't a lot of room at the top,
and the farther up you go, the more
you have to decide which friends
you're gonna leave behind. I didn't
bail on her. She bailed on me."
She turns and looks at me.
"For that matter, so did you."

I take a step back.
"You were better off without me.
I was pretty messed up after Frankie died."

Bri shrugs. "You dumped your friends
to be pathetic and depressed. I'll give Ally credit.
At least she did it for popularity."

BRIANNA LEAVES

and I sit down on the ledge to
think about what she said
as I watch kids scurry
to and fro.

A fight breaks out
near Vo-Tech.
Two girls make out
secretly.

A dead boy stands
yelling in the midst
of it all, and nobody
sees him but
me.

BIRD'S-EYE VIEW

The main campus is an octagon
of eight brick buildings
with the gym at one end
and Watchdog Tower at the other.

Humanities, the library,
and the cafeteria are to the north.
Sci-Tech, Vo-tech, and the
FAB are to the south.

The quad is a patchwork
of sidewalks and grass.
The dead boy stands on the circle
in the middle of it all,
on top of the big, black bird
painted on the concrete.

Seniors beat you up
if you step on the mascot.
They think they're teaching
the freshmen school respect.

There are way more
buildings than necessary,
lots of empty rooms,
and half a dozen locations
where no one ever goes.
Kids make up great stories
to explain the reasons why.
Nobody understands
that it's because

those places are dead zones.

I'M STILL PRETTY MESSED UP

How can I explain to Bri
that I distance myself because
if I get too close, people will think
I'm crazy and I'll get locked up again?
If the doctors knew the truth
about me, they might not
let me out next time.

I'm not crazy, but I can't tell
anybody except for my new
best friend, Oscar Smith.

He sees dead people too.
This school is full of them.

THE NINE CIRCLES OF RAVEN VALLEY HIGH

There's an abandoned football field
up on the hill that looks down
on the new stadium.
It's filled with soldiers from some
obscure Civil War battle that didn't
make it into the history books.

Day after day,
boys barely older than me
fight the same war.
Night after night,
they lie bloody on the grass.
Every now and then,
when one of them is ready
to cross over,
a raven comes
to take him
to the next world.

There used to be a courthouse
where the old gym stands.
They hanged murderers
and horse thieves
on the steps.
That's where the
violent offenders go.

As for their victims,
they occupy the

dusty prop room
in the basement
under the theater.

There's a dark corner
in the cafeteria
reserved for those
who starved to death.
Two members
from a family of early settlers
who didn't store enough
food for the winter
and an anorexic cheerleader
from the nineties.
An abandoned ropes course
is home to the foolhardy,
and the weight room
at the back of the gym
is for the jocks
who still can't believe
they died in their prime.

The administration building is
a melting pot
of those who succumbed
to fatal diseases,
broken hearts, and
people who just got stuck
for no apparent reason.

Not good. Not bad.
Just too mediocre
to continue on.

The Raptor Circle is home to the one person
who died from an act of God.

As for the H Hall,
I spent a week there last spring,
when I went up to the old football field
and swallowed that bottle of pills.

When I was in middle school,
Frankie used to take me
up on the hill
to see the games.

Now all I watch
are dead people.

From this perspective,
it's like viewing
a theater in the round.

THE STAGE

If it's true
that all the school's a stage
and we are merely players,
what's the purpose of our plans,
of our struggles, of our prayers?

And is there any chance that
we might get to write the script?
Even just for one last scene.
To have a little bit

of self-determination.
Could that have been your goal?
Reaching for the one last thing
that put you in control

of how the story ended.
If I could plan our lives,
it wouldn't be a tragedy.
If I could pen our lines,
it would be quite different.
I'd give you another chance
to throw away the sloppy copy
and write a second draft.

But I don't get to write your story.
I must leave that up to you.
I just hope you understand,
it isn't through.

PART FIVE

"<u>N</u>O _ <u>X</u>I<u>T</u>"
<u>A</u> <u>T</u>RA<u>G</u>_<u>D</u>Y
<u>I</u>N O<u>N</u>_ RASH
A<u>C</u>T

Ally

CAST OF CHARACTERS

Ally .... Me

Sister .... Quiet Girl in Black

Julie Ann .... Doomed Lover

Rotceo .... Another Doomed Lover

Hangman .... Ruler of the Hallway

INT. HALLWAY—EARLY MORNING

I wake to the sound of birds cooing. Sit up. Look out the window at the awning to see the pigeons huddled together against the cold. Remember I'm still on the hallway. Must have stayed here all night, though I don't remember anything beyond the last bell.

I wonder what would happen if one of the birds got pushed out of the flock. I see the raven sitting on the railing and I know the answer. The world is a cruel place for those on their own.

Slowly, dawn approaches and kids start arriving. I rub my right shoulder, stiff from sleeping all night on the tile bench.

SISTER
You get used to it.

I jump, surprised to find a girl dressed in black sitting on the tile bench and knitting. She's wearing a long-sleeved dress that looks like it went out of style in the 1960s, or maybe even the 1860s—if it ever was in style. There are flowers braided into her hair: white narcissus and blue forget-me-nots from down by the river. Something about the blue flowers tugs at my memory, but I don't know why.

SISTER
After a while you don't feel a thing.

ALLY
What are you talking about?

SISTER

The pain.

I'm irritated at the intrusion. The hallway is my haven. But I also get the feeling from her tone that this girl knows something I don't.

ALLY

You spent the night here too?

SISTER
(without looking up from her knitting)
I spend every night here.

I wonder if she's homeless. Am surprised to find I really don't care. The hallway feels as cold as ice, but the cold doesn't bother me. Nothing bothers me, not even the strange girl in black. Let her sit there. I don't care.

A teacher hurries through the hallway carrying a stack of copies from the workroom. Almost runs into me. I have to jump out of the way to keep from getting run over.

SISTER

To them we're invisible.

ALLY

Yeah. Tell me about it.

It reminds me of my father's golden rule: Kids are meant to be seen and not heard. Preferably not seen, either. It's why Dad built me my own entertainment room on the back of the house. He doesn't care what goes on in there as long as he can't see it or hear it or smell it.

A dozen teachers hurry through the hallway with their stacks of copies, and I sit on the tile bench to avoid getting trampled.

When the tardy bell rings, I'm irritated to see an ROTC guy and his girlfriend making out at the other end of the hallway.

ALLY

Hey! Get a room. If everybody starts ditching here, security is gonna notice.

The ROTC dude doesn't hear me. His girlfriend tries to answer but she can't. The guy's tongue is too far down her throat. And what's with that outfit she's wearing? Is the hallway some sort of hideaway for the social misfits of Raven Valley High?

ALLY

I said . . . security is going to notice.

HANGMAN

Nobody's going to notice.

I turn to see a guy in a thrift store coat two sizes too big hovering over me. His jeans are full of holes. Not stylish Hollister holes. Someone has tried to patch his up, but even his patches have holes. If he's embarrassed by his appearance, he doesn't show it. He towers over me like he's trying to intimidate me, which isn't working.

ALLY

Can I help you?

HANGMAN

Yeah. You're sitting in my spot.

Now I'm really irritated.

ALLY

Do you own this hall?

HANGMAN

Actually, I do.

He puts his hand on the wall above my head and leans over me like he's trying to use his size to scare me.

ALLY

I don't see your name anywhere.

The girl in black looks up like she's surprised to hear someone talking back to the Hulk. In truth, I'm surprised too. I've never stood up to anyone. Never sassed my parents. Never confronted the guy at Pizza Barn when he gave me incorrect change. Never told Brianna I wanted to play Guitar Hero when she insisted on DDR. I don't even recognize the voice coming out of my lips. I like it, though. Something about the hallway has made me bolder.

ALLY

I know your type. You're just a garden-variety bully.

HANGMAN

And you're just a garden-variety whore. Did you really think the big football player was going to leave his pretty girlfriend for you?

His words should cut me in two, but they don't, and the fact that they don't is strange. The only explanation is that I just don't care what this loser thinks. It feels invigorating not to care. Feels so terrific, in fact, that I start to laugh. This really pisses off the Hulk, who glares at me until his eyes are like two blue ice cubes.

All at once the room is a freezer, and the cold that didn't faze me before becomes unbearable. The tile beneath my butt is a sheet of ice that grows so cold it burns. I jump to my feet, and when I turn around, the Hulk is reclining on the spot where I was just sitting, head cocked up on his arm, smirking. Makeout girl stands at the opposite end of the hallway, watching us.

JULIE ANN
You're new here.

HANGMAN
(to Julie Ann)
She was here all day yesterday, which you might
have noticed if you hadn't been sucking face for
eight straight hours.

The girl in black glances up at me, and the pink yarn on her lap looks like a dead poodle. She's almost done with her knitting project—a sweater that's about ten sizes too small.

SISTER
(softly)
It's easy to lose track of time.

The Hulk sits up and makes a sweeping gesture with his arm toward the girl in black.

HANGMAN

Alley Cat, meet Little Sister. And down the hallway
we have Rotceo and Julie Ann Fries.

The ROTC guy grabs the hand of the girl in bell bottoms, and pulls her
back onto the bench seat.

ROTCEO

Come back, baby. I need you.

HANGMAN

So what do you think, Alley Cat? Do you like our
accommodations?

ALLY

Why are you calling me that?

HANGMAN

Alley Cats always land on their feet. You can toss
'em off the roof headfirst, but it's their little toes
that always hit the pavement before anything else.

For some reason this causes me to look outside at the yellow crime-scene
tape and wonder if someone has been pushed off the roof.

ALLY

Why do I get the feeling you speak from experience?

HANGMAN
(shrugging)

Some cats want to go off the roof.

ALLY

And you're just the guy to help them.

He smiles as a security guard in a red T-shirt steps onto the H Hall. I look at the ROTC dude, who doesn't even try to hide the fact that he has both hands up his girlfriend's shirt.

We're all going to be caught. My only solace is knowing I'll be sent to in-school suspension instead of back to class.

HANGMAN

He won't bother us.

ALLY

How can you be so sure?

The security guard stops in the middle of the hallway and takes a referral form out of his back pocket.

HANGMAN

Watch.
(walking up behind the security guard)
Keep walking, mister. Hear no evil. See no evil.

The security guard quickly pockets the referral form and hurries out of the hallway.

ALLY

Wow! That was impressive. I don't even think
Will Jones could get away with that.

HANGMAN

Stick around, Alley Cat. I'm just getting started.

SISTER

You really shouldn't encourage him.

She sounds afraid of him, but I'm not. Actually, I find him as intriguing as he is repulsive. I don't know many people who say exactly what's on their minds.

ALLY

You've introduced me to everyone else. What's your name?

HANGMAN

I'm the Hangman, at your service.

ALLY

Strange name. Why do they call you that?

HANGMAN

I like to hang out and I like to play games. How about *Wheel of Fortune*? Wanna take a spin?

SISTER

You *really* shouldn't encourage him.

HANGMAN

Don't listen to her. Too much time in Catholic girls' school. Total party pooper. Would you like to buy a vowel?

While he's been talking, the Hangman has drawn a stick gallows on the wall in red Magic Marker with four blank lines underneath. Great. When security catches us, they can add vandalism to our list of offenses.

HANGMAN

And since you're new to the hallway, I'll even give you a hint. Four-letter word starting with *F*.

SISTER

Oh my!

HANGMAN

"OOOOO my" is exactly right. You've just bought yourself two *O*'s.

He writes two *O*'s after the *F*.

SISTER

No. *No!* I didn't say I wanted to buy a vowel.

HANGMAN

Too late.

ALLY

What does a vowel cost?

The girl in black presses her lips together and shakes her head. She tries to say something, but she can't seem to get any words out. The sweater she's been working on for the past hour unravels, and then the pink yarn floats up to her lips and stitches them together.

ALLY

What's happening?

HANGMAN

Told you she was a party pooper.

ALLY

What did you do to her?

HANGMAN

Don't worry. It doesn't hurt. Now give me a
consonant. That won't cost you anything. Unless
you get it wrong.

ALLY
(standing and moving toward the door)

I don't want to play this game.

HANGMAN
(yelling)

Give me a consonant!

The whole building seems to shake with the thunder of his voice.

ALLY

What's happening?

HANGMAN
(screaming now)

GIVE . . . ME . . . A . . . CONSONANT!

JULIE ANN
(calling from the other end of the hall)
D.

The Hangman turns and glares at Julie Ann.

HANGMAN
Not fair when you've played the game before,
Miss Fries.

She shudders and looks away like she's expecting to get hit, but all the Hangman does is write the letter *D* up on the wall and erase the stick gallows with his sleeve. When the gallows disappears, the pink yarn disentangles itself from the lips of Little Sister.

HANGMAN
F-O-O-D. Rule number one. No food on the hallway.

I look around at the four strangers and realize they are exactly that—strangers. They're all odd enough to have stood out on the quad, but I've never noticed any of them.

ALLY
Who are you guys? What is this place?

HANGMAN
Don't you know?

I look outside at the yellow tape in front of the Fine Arts Building and wonder what happened there. Brady Theater is taller than anything else on campus. There's a ladder leading up to the top and sometimes kids sneak up there to get stoned. I went up there one night with Davis after a football game. I went up there with Darla when she introduced the freshman Ravenettes to Jim Beam. I remember having a huge fight with Dad and thinking it would be a good place to hide.

ALLY

I went up there.

HANGMAN

Ah, yes. It's coming back to her now.

What happened after that is a blur. Was it hours later, or maybe days when someone else was up there with me? I can't seem to remember. All I remember is a voice saying *You'd be better off dead* over and over and over again. *You'd be better off dead. You'd be better off dead. You'd be better off dead. . . .*

ALLY

I went to the edge of the roof.

HANGMAN

And then . . .

ALLY

I went to the edge of the roof because I thought I was going to vomit. I leaned over the side and I got dizzy. I lost my balance and I . . .

HANGMAN

Yes?

ALLY

I fell.

HANGMAN

Is that how you remember it? As I recall, you tried
to go headfirst. Landed on your feet. I was worried
there for a while, but you still managed to knock
your head against the pavement. Might have been
really nasty otherwise.

ALLY

No. That's not what happened. I didn't mean to do it.
I feel sick. I have to get out of here.

I run to the door leading out to the G Hall, but it's locked. I run to the
elevator, but I don't have a key. I run to the window and pound my
fists on the glass, but no one hears me. Then I see the letters from
the exit sign falling to the ground . . .

one by one.

ALLY

What is this place?

HANGMAN

Oh, goody, she wants to play another round.

The Hangman draws another gallows on the wall, and I realize that the
red ink is coming not from a pen but from his finger.

SISTER

You really should try not to ask him questions.

HANGMAN

Four-letter word, starting with *H*. Would you like to buy a vowel?

JULIE ANN

L.

HANGMAN
(tersely)

It's not your turn, Miss Fries.
(composing himself)

But Alley Cat is new here and she obviously needs some help, so I'll let it slide. This time.

He writes the letters on the wall. H __ L L.

ALLY

No! It can't be.

HANGMAN

Yes, it can.

ALLY

This place is hell, isn't it? I'm dead, aren't I? I've died and gone to hell.

HANGMAN

Would you like to solve the puzzle, or do you want to buy a vowel?

I turn to the girl in black.

                    ALLY
          Or maybe it's just purgatory.

She looks away.

                  HANGMAN
          Too many letters. Are you ready to solve the
          puzzle?

I sit on the tile bench and start to cry. I feel an arm around my shoulders
and realize that Julie Ann has come to sit beside me.

                  JULIE ANN
          This place isn't as bad as it seems.

                    ALLY
          I really am in hell, aren't I?

                  HANGMAN
          Is that your final answer?

                   SISTER
          (nervously raising her hand)
          Excuse me.

The Hangman looks at the girl in black with irritation.

                  HANGMAN
     Yes.

SISTER

I'd like to buy an *A*.

HANGMAN
(in irritation)

Fine, then. Have it your way.

The yarn spins itself into a giant pink web with the girl wrapped up in a fuzzy cocoon in the middle. The Hangman adds an *A*.

HANGMAN

H-A-L-L.

The bell for second period rings, and kids start flooding through the G Hall and out of the building. Julie Ann takes my hand and leads me to the window. On the quad below I see Davis and Darla kissing under a tree.

JULIE ANN

Don't try to make it complicated.
(she points outside)

That—is high school.

That—is hell.

This is just the hallway.

THINGS THAT FALL

Night
   falls.
Water
    falls.

Snow falls, soft and wet,
   gathering on tree branches
     and dirty streets.

People fall
   in love,
     out of love,
       to sleep.

Sometimes they even fall
          from
            rooftops.

   And sometimes

      they
        j

            u

                m

                  p

PART SIX

LIFE
(OR IS IT DEAT_?)
IN T_E
_ALLWAY

Ally

FIRE OR ICE

Here's a
truth
that I have
learned—

ice
can be
so cold

it burns.

SISTER SISYPHUS

sits knitting
hour after hour

little spider fingers
work at the yarn

knit one
purl two
knit one
purl two

every time she
reaches
the final
row

it

u
n
r
a
v
e
l
s

a
t

h
e
r

f
e
e
t

THE GIRL IN BLACK KNITS

another pink sweater. Smiles.
Holds it up when she

is done. I notice the bump
under her dress. "You're pregnant."

She puts a hand on
her stomach. "When I told one
of the other girls

about the baby, she said
I wasn't the only one.

She told me I could
hide it under my robes, and
afterward, I could

put it in the river that
ran through the convent, but I

couldn't bear the thought
of leaving my sweet, helpless
baby there alone.

So one dark night before she
was born, I filled my pockets

with rocks, went down to
the water, and I never
came back out again."

WHILE ROTCEO SLEEPS

Julie Ann comes and sits
beside me.

She presses her back
against the wall like she's trying to
make herself invisible.

For the longest time
she doesn't say a word. Sits
as still as a bird.

"When he wakes up, don't tell him
where I am. I'm sick of him."

There's no place to hide,
but I let it pass. She seems
so tired and desperate.

"Eternal Love isn't what
the poets claim it to be."

"Just say no," I tell the girl.

"I can't. He did it for me.
They were going to
send him away to the war.
I couldn't live without him.

We used to meet at the headmaster's house
when he and his family were out of town.
It was right behind the dormitories.
I knew where the key was hidden
because I babysat his kids."

She looks back at the boy in fatigues.

"He was beautiful.
The first time we made love it
was in a bathtub.

Him
and me
and a hair dryer."

DEAD END

"That was the end of me.

He lasted another week.
Ended it with a forty-five.

We swore we'd be
together
for eternity,

but when you're
seventeen,
you have no
idea
how long
that can be."

LET'S PLAY ANOTHER GAME

the Hangman says.
He seems to have a thing
for four-letter words.
This one starts with *C*.

No one is willing
to buy a vowel.

He soon gives up and writes
the word C-A-K-E
on the wall.

Rule number two
of the hallway:
"You can't have your cake
and eat it too."

"You already told us there's no
food," I remind him.

"Not that kind of cake," he says,
pointing at Rotceo and Julie Ann,
who are at it again.

You can have all the love
you want but it will never
be enough.

THE TANTALIZING DUO

does a dance
on the floor.

When she tries
to break away,
his lips whisper
More.

If she tries
to take a breath,
he smothers her
with kisses.

His hands are
never far
from her pale, white
skin.

She finally sighs
in resignation

and lets
him win.

I CAN'T BELIEVE

I've ended up here,
with these pitiful people.

I wanted to do
something with my life.
I wanted to be somebody.

Was that a sin?

I tried out for the lead in *My Fair Lady,*
and I would have nailed it except for the fact
that Darla was a senior and I was just a freshman.
"You'll have lots of opportunities," Mrs. Salazar told me.

But it didn't feel like that.
It felt like my life was over.

I was assigned the role of a flower seller,
but I've never been good at being just
one of the crowd.

After the parts were posted,
Darla took the Ravenettes
up on the roof of Brady Theater
to celebrate.

I wanted to go home and hide.
Everyone knew I'd gone up
against Darla for the lead,
and lost.

I would have gone home,
if I hadn't been so afraid
of what they would say about me
in my absence.

I was glad I didn't, because
when we arrived, Davis
and the guys from the football team
were already there.
Darla was instantly on him
like a lioness in heat.

Davis tried not to look in my direction,
but he kept stealing glances,
especially when Will Jones draped his arm
around me and started drinking a bottle of Jim Beam.

"If we get caught with alcohol, we'll all be on a
forty-five-day activity suspension," whined one
of the freshman girls.

"Then don't be stupid enough to get caught," said Darla.

I felt sorry for them, for how afraid they looked,
huddled together like pigeons
seeking the protection of the roost.

Darla grabbed the Jim Beam from Will
and took a drink.

She handed it to me,
her eyes daring me to defy her,
the way I'd defied her by trying out for her part.

There was an unwritten rule that nobody went up against Darla.
But there's a problem with unwritten rules.
Nobody can read them.
Not that I would have paid attention to that one.

I looked her straight in the eyes,
grabbed the whiskey from her hand,
and took a long, slow swallow.
It tasted like my father's aftershave and burned
all the way down my throat.
I wanted to gag and vomit, but I didn't dare.

Darla seemed pleased.
She took the bottle from me
and handed it back to Will.
Then she leaned in close and whispered,
"Don't worry about the play, Ally.
When I'm gone, you can be
the queen of everything."

It seemed I had been forgiven.
And in a few minutes, a warm,
buzzing sensation washed over my entire body.
I didn't care how bad the stuff tasted,
I wanted more.
So I grabbed the bottle and took another long drink.

The other freshman girls slinked away, and Darla laughed
as she watched them scurrying down the fire escape.
"Lightweights," she called after them.

Darla called up the sound track from *Chicago*
on her iPod, and a few of us got up
to do our dance routine while Darla directed us
from the sidelines.

When we got to the part where
we typically unzipped our Windbreakers,
in a mock striptease,
we took off our shirts instead.

"Hey, freshman," Will called out to me. "Take it all off."

I loved the way he and the other boys
suddenly turned their attention to me.

I loved the way Davis's eyes filled with
panic as I reached to unhook my bra.
And I loved the way Davis suddenly
sprang up from where he was sitting,
put his arm around me, and turned me away
from the other guys.

He handed me my shirt and told the others,
"Don't mess with Ally, she's Bri's friend.
I'm taking her home."

"Good," said Darla. "We wouldn't want her to miss her curfew."

"Stay away from Will," Davis warned
when we got to the bottom of the ladder.
"He's trouble."

"He's your best friend," I said,
pretending to slump so he had to hold me up.

"That's how I know he's trouble."

When we got to his car, Davis started the engine,
and he drove about a block before he had to
throw on the brakes, because I'd unzipped his pants.
He pushed my hand away. "Damn it, Ally.
Do you want to get us both killed?"

"What I want is you."

"You're drunk."

"I still want you."

I reached for him again, and he tried to push me away,
but I pulled up my skirt and crawled on top of him.

I loved how bold the liquor made me feel.
And I loved how we made love,
right there in the car,
under the streetlight.

Just a block away from where
Darla was celebrating her victory.

HOMECOMING DRESS

Darla broke up with Davis
two weeks later. It was five days
before homecoming when they had
a huge fight on the quad.
She said she was tired of him
tying her down.

He asked me to the dance that same night.
"We can go out to my car between sets,"
he said, like he wanted me to do for him
what I'd done the night I got
drunk on the roof.

Truth is, I would have done anything
he wanted.

I was so elated, I spent
every dime I had on a
red silk gown and shoes.

Megan Frost, one of the other freshman
Ravenettes, helped me choose it.

She was dying to know
who my date was, but Davis
said we should keep it quiet
until homecoming night.

I couldn't wait to see the looks
on the faces of the other girls
when they saw me with him.

But the secret was burning
a hole in me,
so I confided in Brianna
and asked her to come
with me and Megan to the mall.

"To help you get ready for a date with the Thing,
yeah, right."

Screw her. I didn't need
her self-righteous BS in my life.

I'd completely forgotten about the photo
she'd taken. Had no idea she'd want revenge.

For three days I couldn't eat a thing.
On Wednesday afternoon,
at the pep rally, my heart swelled
when Davis was elected king.
I was just a freshman,
and I was going to the dance
with the homecoming king!

So what if I didn't get to play
Eliza Doolittle.
I was becoming the star
of my own life.

But then Darla was chosen queen,
and my victory began to feel tentative.

Somewhere between the
gymnasium and the parking lot,
Darla decided it would be
awkward if she and Davis didn't
go to the dance
together. So they sort of
patched things up.

I was devastated.
I'd lost my only chance
to be with Davis at homecoming.
Next year he would be far away at
college. He said he was sorry. He hadn't
planned for things to turn out this way.
He said if I went to the dance,
he and I could still
hook up in the parking garage.

The parking garage!

I couldn't go. I couldn't face
seeing him with her again.

When Friday came, I stayed home sick,
crying half the day, and then
I got the scissors from the drawer,
cut and shredded, ripped and tore.
Red silk covered half the floor.
Then Will Jones called me on the phone.
He said he'd heard that I was free.
Would I like to double with him
and Davis and Darla?

I said, "Yes,"
thrilled that Davis had found a way
for us to be together.

I tried to put the red silk pieces back,
but a gown is like a broken heart.
So easy to tear it apart;
hard to put it together again.

BACKFIRE

When I showed up at the local
Steak and Ale
with Will, and we slipped
into the booth, Davis grew pale,
but Darla didn't seem the least
surprised.

When Will and Darla went
to talk with friends,
Davis said, "What the hell
are you doing here with him?"

"Isn't that what you wanted?" I asked.

"Are you out of your mind?" he replied.

That was the first moment
I remember
ever wanting to die.

THE COCKTAIL

When Darla came back to the table,
she grabbed me by the arm and told the boys,
"Ally and I are going to the restroom."

I was so afraid she'd found out about me
and Davis that I felt cold sweat trickle down my spine.
Was she going to corner me in the bathroom
and nail me to the wall?

When we got inside, she pushed me
into a huge handicapped stall,
and I was surprised to find three
other Ravenettes waiting there.
Maybe they'd all get a piece of me.

But they didn't even glance my way.
They just took prescription pill
bottles out of their purses,
obviously stolen from home,
and emptied them into a Styrofoam
to-go box.

Darla shook up the contents
like microwave popcorn.
Then she opened the lid
and everybody took a handful.

She pushed the box toward me.
I shook my head.
Whiskey was one thing,
but we could end up dead.
This was
Russian roulette.
I pictured myself overdosing
and nobody being able to tell
the doctors what I'd taken.

Darla pushed the box toward me,
more insistently.
"If you want to play with the big girls,
then *play* with the big girls."

"No!" I said.

"I told you she was a wuss,"
said Lauren Payne, Darla's second-in-command.

Darla rolled her eyes
like I was a little child.
"It's nothing dangerous, Ally.
We're not stupid.
It's just something to keep us going.
You don't want to be falling asleep
when the party's just getting started."

I still hesitated.

"Or maybe you do.
Never mind."

She started to pull the box away,
and I heard myself say, "Wait!"

If she could do it, I could do it.
So I took a handful of pills.
Washed them down
while the other girls stared.

It was only later,
very much later,
that it dawned on me—
I never saw them
swallow theirs.

HOW IT HAPPENED

I remember Dad yelling
when I got home.
He could tell I was stoned.
His words were a hammer beat,
inside my head.
Had to get out of there.
Ran to the school.

Was that how I ended up dead?
Was I so messed up
in the head that I walked
off the roof of the FAB?
Why don't I remember that?

Maybe you don't have to do it
on purpose to get here.

"If you're all suicides,
then what's your story?"
I ask the Hangman.
"You don't seem like
the self-destructive type."

"I'm not," he replies. "I fell.
Unfortunately
I had a rope around my
neck at the time."

"Who put it there?" I ask.

"I did. But I didn't want to die.
I just wanted to get somebody's
attention. You know all about that,
don't you, Ally?"

I remember the dance.
How the floor seemed to spin.
How I was afraid I'd take off and fly away.
How I wanted strong hands to hold me down.
How I let Will rub himself on me
because I hoped Davis would see,
but he just kept ignoring me.

So when Will asked if
I wanted to go outside
to get some air,
I said yes, because I needed
room to think and I had
to get the hell out of there.

"I didn't really want to die,"
I tell the Hangman,
though I still
can't remember why
I jumped.

"I didn't want to die either," he says.
"It doesn't matter. I'm still dead.
But don't underestimate me.
I'm not like the rest of them."

OSCAR SMITH & WESSON

It's that special ed
teacher again,
pushing Oscar Smith
across the floor.

He contorts
and utters
a silent scream
that the teacher
never hears.

Looks
right at the Hangman.
Oscar's eyes fill with fear.

"Can he see us?" I ask.

"Of course he can,"
says the Hangman.
Grabbing Oscar's head,
he turns it toward me.

"Oscar Smith and Wesson
used to be a resident
of this hall,
but he didn't have
the balls to stay."

Oscar tries to pull away,
and that's when
I see it—
the dent in his head
where the bullet
made its intrusion
into his skull.

The Hangman laughs
as Oscar is rolled away,
crying.

"Remember, Ally,
there are worse things
than dying."

PART SEVEN

A_OTHER SLEEPLESS _IGHT

Elijah

MY HOUSE

Back in my room I lie awake all night,
tossing, turning. Getting out of bed,
I look out the window at the sky,

say a silent prayer, and bang my head
against the glass. Hear my father's voice
as he complains about the cost of bread,

ingratitude, why Mom can't make a choice
to leave the couch. She's stuck to it like glue.
I hear him threaten he'll use some force

to get her moving. Says he'll show her who
is boss. I hear him stumble as he falls
into a chair, too drunk to follow through.

I sneak out of my room and down the hall.
Heading for the door, I hear him cry.
Hear him whisper even as he bawls,

*If there really is a God, then why
did Frankie have to be the one to die?*

WHY?

Why did Frankie have to be the one
to die? He was the family's golden child.
Beloved brother, athlete, student, son.

Would they be happy for a little while
if I died too? I think about Mom's feet,
as they faltered on the cold, white tile—

her hand, as she laid it on my sheet,
her thin lips as she whispered, "Please don't go."
The crying of a voice filled with defeat.

I made a choice to come back. Should have known,
to them it couldn't matter. Didn't make
their lives the least bit better. They don't show

the slightest sign they're glad I didn't take
the easy way out. God knows I have tried
to make it up to them, but I can't shake

the feeling that my mother may have lied
to herself when she wept for me that day.
Their lives would be so simple if I'd died.

That's too damn bad, Dad, 'cause I'm here to stay,
and here's something I would really like
for you to ponder when you feel this way.

The reason my brother isn't here tonight
is because Frankie *chose* to end his life.

THE CURVE

Frank, big bro, I'd really like to know
what you were feeling on that day in March
when you decided you just had to leave.
You couldn't stay another minute more.
They told us that you took the curve too fast,
went flying over rock and cliff and rail.
It happened on that dark and lonely road
where the girl you loved had met her end.
Your pencil left no mark on the page
to tell us why you thought you had to go.
Your tires left no marks on the road,
but your absence leaves a hole in all our lives.

I overheard our father ask the cop
if he thought you even tried to stop.

DEAR FRANK

Remember how our mother used to be?
She's gotten worse since you've gone away.
She lies on the couch and smokes and drinks.
She sleeps there, eats there, seldom showers now.
Talk show hosts are her only friends.
Dad works late at the shop, and then
he comes home drunk and slips into his den
of ratchets, wrenches, pinup poster girls.

As for me, I took some sleeping pills.
That didn't work out quite the way I'd planned.
I guess I really didn't want to die.
There are still some things I'd like to do,
a special girl I'd really like to know.

You said you'd never leave me here alone,
even if it meant you had to wait
another year for me to graduate.
You were going to be an engineer.
I would make my living on the stage.
I'd study Shakespeare and direct some plays.
I'd get a role in *Streetcar*. You would sit
right up in front and cheer me at the close.
We'd be the first ones in our family
to go to college, visit NYC,
fly in a plane, make something of our lives.
Stay sober long enough to see the world.

I feel my life unraveling like yarn.
The strands come loose, and then they fly away.
What happens when I reach the end of it?
Make a knot and hold on, or let go?

FOLLOW THE LEADER

Dear Frank, I think about when I was ten.
I'd follow you to soccer practice; then
I'd follow you to hang out with the guys,
who called me Shadow, but you didn't care

that every time you turned, you saw me there
studying you, hoping I could watch
you long enough to imitate your walk,
your stride, your talk, your manliness, your air.

I tried to follow you to the science fair.
Turned out that wasn't quite the gig for me,
but I stuck behind you when you joined
the band and went with you to music camp.

When you missed that curve, did it cross your mind,
that I might
                be following
                            behind?

HEY, BRO

Dear Frank, you were the guy I counted on
to tell me what you thought I ought to do.
Ally slipped away so far, I doubt
she will make it back without some help.
She'll need someone to show her the way out
of the dark and hopeless place she's gone to.
Do you think I'm supposed to be the one?

I hoped if I waited long enough,
Ally would get tired of Davis and
his fame, his game, his lame attempts at "cool."
Eventually she'd see it was an act,
that there was nothing beneath the mask
but self-obsession. I'd be ready when
she finally realized she wanted more
from life, from love—that she had settled for
someone who loved himself, and self alone.
She'd look around and she would finally see
someone who really loved her. Me.

ADVICE

I really need some brotherly advice,
to figure out what I'm supposed to do.
I feel your presence haunting every room,
and yet you never give me any sign.
I talk to you and never hear a response.
I write to you and never get a reply.
I go out to the road, the place you died.
I cannot find you and I wonder why
I can see the souls around the school,
the place where I tried to end my life,
but out here on the road where you went down,
I never even get a glimpse of you.

I yell at you and scream and rant and rave,
but you are just as silent as the grave.

PART EIGHT

"N_ EXIT"
SCENE TW_

Ally

CAST OF CHARACTERS

Ally
afraid, alone
hurting, hiding, biding
never can go back
me

Sister
timid, guarded
sitting, knitting, praying
quiet girl in black
nun

Rotceo
hungry, unsatisfied
holding, kissing, groping
always gets his way
loverboy

Julie Ann
trapped, bored
forgetting, conceding, letting
she never gets away
girlfriend

Hangman
dark, dangerous
playing, plotting, punishing
ruler of the hall
demon

And a cameo appearance by

Elijah
brave, bold
knowing, helping, showing
he risks it all
friend

INT. HALLWAY – LATE AFTERNOON

The last bell has rung, and the students are leaving the buildings, flooding toward the buses. The hallway is quiet now as we all sit, looking out onto the quad at the students hooking up, making plans, calling friends. The students who all still have lives.

SISTER
This is the hardest part.

HANGMAN
Shut up.

JULIE ANN
You get used to it.

ROTCEO
No, you don't.

ALLY
They can all leave, and we never can. We're stuck in high school for eternity. This really is hell.

SISTER
It's not hell. I don't think God would kick us when we're down.

ALLY
Yeah, but you're not sure, are you?

The Hangman strides over to stand in front of me.

HANGMAN

You simpleton. You still don't get it.
(pointing out the window)
Those stupid little bastards think what they have
is a life, but they're dead wrong. It's so pathetic
watching them day after day, making their little
plans, staging their little dramas. They think
they're gonna live forever, but they're already
rotting. They're just too stupid to know it.

SISTER

Leave her alone.

HANGMAN

Why should I? The sooner she faces reality, the
better.

JULIE

You think this is reality?

HANGMAN
(turning back to me)
What did you want when you came here?

ALLY

I don't remember.

HANGMAN

Of course you do. When you were standing on top
of that building thinking about how pathetic your
life was, what did you want?

I wince, expecting the pain of his words to hit me all at once, but they
don't, and I am relieved to find that I really don't care anymore.

ALLY

I must have just wanted to stop hurting.

HANGMAN

And . . .

ALLY

And now I don't feel anything.

The Hangman turns and writes B-I-N-G-O on the wall.

HANGMAN

Rotceo and Julie Ann wanted to be together
forever. Our little sister wanted to *not* drown her
baby. I wanted to be king of the crap hill. What do
they call that place where everybody gets what he
wants?

The Hangman draws an *H* on the wall followed by five blank lines:
H __ __ __ __ __.

HANGMAN
Who wants to buy a vowel?

No one answers.

HANGMAN
Must I do everything myself?

He fills in the letters.

HANGMAN
H-E-A-V-E-N. That's what they call it.

I stand and walk over to the window, where I see Elijah down below on the quad. He looks like a salmon swimming upstream as he pushes his way through the crowd toward the steps of Humanities. He glances up at the second-floor window where I stand and there is something frantic in his eyes.

ALLY
I wonder where he's going.

The Hangman joins me at the window.

HANGMAN
Well, well. If it isn't Sleeping Beauty. I wonder if he has any more pills in his pocket.

Elijah breaks through the crowd. Once he is past the other students, he runs up the steps, taking them two at a time. The girl in black turns and whispers to me . . .

SISTER

He's coming for you.

ALLY

What do you mean?

HANGMAN
(turning on Sister)

Don't you dare say another word.
(to Rotceo)
You know what to do.

Rotceo springs from his seat and moves toward me.

JULIE ANN

No, baby. Just let her be.

He ignores Julie Ann, grabs me, shoves me into a corner, and then
shields me with his body.

I feel like I'm suffocating as I try to push him away, but he's as solid as
a mountain.

ALLY

What are you doing?

ROTCEO

It's for your own protection.

His arms have me pinned to the wall. I look over his shoulder to see
Elijah opening the door that leads onto the H Hall. He stands there but
doesn't come in.

ELIJAH

Ally, where are you? I know you're here.
Oh, God. I hope I'm not too late.

My body feels light and heavy at the same time. My brain, or what used to be my brain, is pounding against my skull in revelation. Elijah knows I'm here! I try to call out to him, but Rotceo puts a hand over my mouth.

ELIJAH
(more urgently)

Ally, if you hear me, let me know.

JULIE ANN

Baby, let her go.

ROTCEO
(to the Hangman)

What do I do with her if he tries to come in?

HANGMAN

He wouldn't dare.

But even as he says it, Elijah takes a cautious step onto the H Hall. He hesitates and then jumps back as if his foot is on fire.

SISTER

She should have the chance to decide.

HANGMAN

She made her decision when she jumped.

Elijah tries again to move onto the hallway: He takes three quick steps inside and then doubles over like someone has punched him in the gut. The Hangman hurries over to him, grabs Elijah's hair, and lifts his head. Terror fills Elijah's eyes.

HANGMAN

I warned you not to ever come back here.

He pushes Elijah against a wall and forces his forearm against Elijah's throat. Meanwhile, Julie Ann tries to pull her boyfriend off me, and the girl in black rocks back and forth, mumbling the Hail Mary.

ELIJAH

Ally, you're not like the rest of them.
If you come with me, you've got a chance.

I look at Julie Ann for an explanation.

JULIE ANN

You're not dead yet.

My heart, or what used to be my heart, pounds like a freight train. I'm not dead. Is there hope for me? Do I want there to be?

The Hangman shoves Elijah out onto the G Hall with such force that he hits his head on the far wall and crumples to the floor. As the door begins to close, Julie Ann is finally able to pull Rotceo off me. I run to the exit. The Hangman lunges for me but falls facedown on the tile. Somehow his feet have become entangled in pink yarn. The girl in black smiles.

HANGMAN

I'm warning you. Don't go out there.

That's hell. This is heav—

But I don't hear the rest of what he says because I'm standing on the G Hall looking at Elijah, and the door has slammed shut behind us.

PART NINE

B_CK IN THE RE_L WORLD

Ally

IT HITS ME

as soon as
I step off
the H Hall.

The air
feels like a thousand
razors
cutting my skin,
filling my lungs
with pieces of glass.

The weight of it
is too much.
I can't walk.
Can't speak.

All I can think about
is returning
to the safety
of the hallway.

I turn back.
Elijah tries to grab
my hand,
but his fingers
go right through me.

"Run!" he yells,
and the force
of his breath
pushes me outside.

Then we're racing
side by side,
down the stairs,
across the yard.

The sunlight
burns my eyes
and the noise
is deafening.

It's like coming
out of the safety
of the womb
to face a cruel,
inhospitable world.

I DON'T KNOW

where we're going;
I just keep following—
running or gliding
or whatever it is
I'm doing.

He keeps looking
behind him to make sure
I'm still there.

The pain throughout
my body is
unbearable,
crushing,
suffocating.

We approach a
line of yellow
school buses,
exhaust fumes
pouring out their
rear ends.

The smell of it
is fire in my nostrils
and down my throat,

or what used to be
my nose and throat.

Elijah stops,
turns away from
the buses
so no one can see
him talking
to a ghost or spirit
or whatever it is
I am now.

"It's gonna be crowded,
so you'll have to sit
on my lap."

"What?" I reply.

He points to Will Jones.
"Unless you want him
walking through you."

I nod my consent.

Will has a pickup,
but he likes to ride the bus
sometimes, so he can
torment the freshmen.

Elijah gets on
and sits in the front.
I slide onto his lap
and he feels warm.

I wonder if he can feel me.
Probably not, but
I almost hope yes.

The bus begins to roll.
There is laughter
and shouting
coming from the back.

Rave on wheels.

I wonder how
the bus driver can
stand it.

Then I see
the earphones.

He's rocking out
to tunes on his
iPod just like
everyone else.

Q & A

"Can you see me?"

                "Yes."

"Can you hear me?"

                "Yes."

"Can you feel me?"

                Pause.

                "Yes, but it's different."

That makes two of us.
I can suddenly feel everything
with painful clarity.

"Why does it hurt so much?"

                "Because it's life. It's intense."

"It sucks."

                "Not all of it."

THE BUS

comes to a stop
in front of a sign that reads
Riverview Estates,
only there are no estates
and no view of the river,
just a bunch of ramshackle houses.

When the county sold the old buildings
to the school district, they subdivided
the surrounding land and put up cheap housing.

We get off and
walk to a house
with broken-down
cars parked all over
the front lawn.

"You live here?" I ask Elijah
as we walk toward the door.

"I prefer to think of it as serving time."
I hear a man yelling from inside the house.
Elijah stops walking.
"Damn. What's he doing home?"

He looks at the front door.
Looks at the cars parked on the lawn.
Walks over to a Camaro
badly in need of a paint job
and opens the door.

Fishes under the
floor mat for a key.
Starts the engine.
"Get in,"
he tells me.

"I didn't know you
had your license."

"I don't,"
he says as we lurch
over the curb and down
the street.

"Where are you taking me?"

"To the hospital, eventually.
But we need to go somewhere
so I can explain things.
Prepare you."

"For what?"

He hesitates.

"For what?" I ask again.

"You're in a coma, Ally.
You've shattered both your legs,
and you might have brain damage.
You're going to have
to make some big decisions.
You need to be prepared."

"Why?"

"It's life. There are no guarantees."
I slink down in the seat of the car.
I'm off the hall, but not
out of the woods.

OSCAR'S HOUSE

We park in an alley
and Elijah opens the gate
to a yard filled with brown
grass and leafless trees,
except for a lone pine
sitting in the middle of
it all, the great green hope.

Elijah walks to the back
door, and I'm surprised to
discover that Oscar's orange
pencil is keeping
the door ajar.
Elijah stoops to pick it up
and I see the words
FREE YOUR MIND
stamped on the side,
right next to the eraser.

"Very funny, Oscar."

"What?"

"Just a reminder
that you can't walk through doors.
Somebody has to leave
one open for you."

I follow Elijah as he walks
down the hall. Hear a woman
in the kitchen singing.
The smell of fried
chicken fills my nostrils.
It's heavenly.

"I'm so hungry," I tell him.

"That's a good sign."

We pass four bedrooms
with music blaring from iPod
docks and radios. A girl
looks up at Elijah from a paperback
novel, then returns to her reading
as if it's no big deal to have some guy
walking through the middle of the
house unannounced. A kid with a
crew cut does pull-ups on a bar
hanging from his door.

"What is this place?" I ask Elijah.

"Treatment foster care," he tells me as he
opens the door to a bedroom
at the end of the hall.

Oscar is sitting in front of a
computer screen that's hooked up
to the device on his wheelchair.
His back is to us and he's clutching
a permanent marker in his fist,
using it to press the keys,
playing chess with someone online.

"Want this back?" Elijah says, handing
Oscar his pencil. Oscar smiles, drops
the marker, grabs the pencil, and
presses another set of keys.
I hear a thick Austrian accent.
I can't believe I have a hot
girl in my bedroom.

"That sounds like the Terminator," I say.

"Yeah, it's a combination of Oscar's
sense of humor and the kind
of stuff you can do with technology.
Watch out. He's a real Casanova."

Oscar looks at me and winks.
At least he tries. It comes out like a squint.
His smile is as big as the room, and I wonder
what he has to smile about. He seemed so
scared and desperate when I saw him on
the hallway.

I can't help but laugh,
even though the entire
scene is so surreal, or
maybe because of that fact.

"He's a real smart-ass
for someone who can't talk,"
Elijah tells me. Then he touches
my hand. "But I'm glad
he makes you smile."

Elijah has stubble on his chin,
which along with the ponytail
and loose white shirt, makes him look
a bit like a pirate.

And I wonder
when he started shaving,
and when he pierced his ears,
and why I didn't try harder to make him
talk to me after his brother died.

THE RULES

Elijah: Oscar:

There are some things you
need to know. Some things you
can't do.

                    Lots of places you can't go . . .

unless a door is left open for you.
Don't try to teleport or walk through walls,
move objects, or talk to people
through their thoughts.

                    You can't bend spoons
                    with your mind.

You can watch and listen and
that's all.

                    No haunting rooms.

You don't have a lot of time.

                    Four days, tops.

After that you would be
too far gone.

Now listen close. When you see
yourself in the hospital, try not to
freak. In half a second . . .

you could lose it all.

Face the pain.
You can't let desperation
shut you down.

Or you'll go right back to the hall.

IT HITS ME

all at once, how very
tired I am, and I can't
help but yawn.

"Sleep," says Elijah.
"You need your rest."

But I'm already sinking
down onto a bean bag chair,
thinking about
how cozy this room feels.

I think about asking Oscar
why he doesn't live with
his parents, but before
I have a chance,
I'm fast asleep.

WHEN I WAKE UP

it's early morning.
In the dark I see
Elijah sitting up.
He's knotting a strand
of blue flowers together and
I wonder where he got them
in the middle of October.
Then I see the pot
of forget-me-nots
on Oscar's windowsill.

Elijah is watching me.
As I look from his face
to the flowers,
I have to catch my breath,
though I don't know why.
He looks away and his
cheeks turn bright red.
I wonder if he sat there all night.

Oscar is fast asleep on the bed.
"He's sweet," I say, because the room
is too quiet.
"He's got attitude."

"That's what I like about him," Elijah says.
"He's got a funny edge for someone who's
been through the things he has."

"What do you mean?"

"He showed the school nurse
the bruises and she called his Mom,
but she just said that Oscar fell a lot.
She covered for his stepdad.

That's when Oscar took the gun out to
the soccer field. Then the cops got involved.
Now his mom sees the stepdad at the pen.
She never sees her son or even emails him."

"That's sad," I say.

"Don't pity him. He hates that.
Peace and happiness are relative."

MORE Q & A

Ally:

Elijah:

You've been on the hallway.

I spent some time there.

When you took those pills.

Not the best move.

How did you end up on the hall?

I did it at the school. Up on the hill.

But you made it back.

It wasn't easy.

How did you get out?

Someone left a door open.

You wanted to die.

I changed my mind.

Why?

I still had some stuff to do.

Like what?

Watch out for you.

You liked me?

I liked the girl I used to know.

I liked her too.

I know you're hurting right now, Ally,
and you may not believe this, but the
pain you feel is temporary. Death
is what lasts forever.

You're right.
I don't believe you.

Give it some time.

WARNING

"The closer you get
to your body,
the more you feel it,"
he tells me.

"Feel what?"

"The pain
that made you
want to give up."

"How do I get back?"

"You have to remember
why you wanted to die.
Then you have to experience
all the pain
and heartache
and disappointment
you ran from before.

Then you have to remember
that it wasn't all bad."

"I remember a few good things,"
I tell him.

"Like what?"

"I remember you."

I REMEMBER THE NIGHT

Elijah
kissed me. I
could tell he wanted
to, but he was so nervous
he wouldn't make the first move.
It was sweet, the way he stood there,
under the streetlight, shifting from foot to
foot, leaning in close and then backing away.
I finally pulled him next to me and he wrapped
me in his arms. His lips, soft as rose petals, searching
out mine. I felt something inside of me burst open, like the
first blossom of spring. I took his hand, led him to a tree, and we
lay down in the grass. Hands exploring lips, lips exploring fingers, and
other things, but not so far that we couldn't turn back. Bodies in motion. Then
we just held each other, under the silent stars. Neither one of us wanted to leave. I
wanted so badly for him to call me that summer, but I knew he wouldn't. He was still
too fragile after what had happened to his brother. I could have called him. I almost did. But

then Davis and I
hooked up. And
afterward nothing
else   mattered.

THE HOSPITAL

It's six a.m. and still dark when
Elijah drives me to the hospital.

We go inside and he walks
up to the nurses' station
to find out where they're keeping me.

ICU, the nurse tells him, but he can't
go in because he's not family.

"You'll have to find your own way in, but I'll
be waiting here."

"What do I do when I get there?"

"Think about your choices.
Feel your feelings.
Remember it wasn't all bad."

He goes to sit in the waiting room,
and I see my father perched in the corner,
coffee in one hand,
cell phone in the other,
laptop and daily planner
on the table in front of him.
He's created a mobile office for himself.

It's good to see I haven't disrupted
his schedule. There's hell to pay
when he gets off his routine.
Mom used to say it kept him
grounded, though that's not
what I would call it.

"Go," Elijah tells me,
but I can't stop staring
at my father.

"Go!" Elijah tells me
a second time,
and I turn and
walk down the hall.

I slip into the ICU
behind a nurse
and begin
looking behind the
curtains,
searching for myself.

THE RESIDENTS OF ICU

There's an old woman
lying on a bed. White hair
flowing across the

pillow. An old man sits next to her,
holds her hand, and weeps, and I

wonder how people
have the guts to stay so long
on such an angry

planet. In the next room there's
a gunshot wound, but no one

sits with him. After
that, the survivors of a
head-on collision

in rooms three and four. Guess that's
what happened to me. I crashed.

THE GIRL IN WHITE

I watch
the girl lying there
in the white room
with the white sheets.
She's in a gown
that looks
like faded wallpaper.

Her skin is
the color of frost

except for
the bruised eyes
sitting like two
moons
sinking into the night

and the blue
vein where the
needle pumps
her full of drugs
like she's a flat tire
in need of air,
only there are
too many holes
to hold it in.

It takes a minute
before I realize
this is me.

BRUISED

When I see Nana
holding the girl's hand,
the pain hits me
like a thousand
razor-sharp blades
cutting me
to pieces.

That's what they did to me.
Hacked away at me
piece
by
piece

until I didn't recognize myself anymore.

I look so damaged—
the bruised apple at
the bottom of the barrel—
and I wonder if there is enough
good left to make it
worth saving.

My father walks in and
he can barely look at me.
"I'm not having
any luck," he says.

"Come sit with Ally," Nana tells him.

He takes a step backward,
toward the door. "I have to keep
working," he says, and
then he's gone.

He's worried about luck
when I'm barely hanging on.
I don't understand him.
I may have gone over the edge,
but there must have been people
who gave me the nudge,
and I'm pretty sure he was one of them.

It feels like the walls
are bearing down on me.
I can't breathe.
I can't bear the pressure.

I can't stay.

I FOLLOW

my father back out
to the waiting room,
where he returns to his
porta-office.

Takes all the pens
out of his briefcase
and lines them up
on the table
with their tips
all pointing due north
and the word
CROSS pointed south.

This is what he does
for relaxation.
He organizes things.
Sometimes it's the pens.
Sometimes it's the peas
and carrots in the pantry.
Sometimes it's me.
Some people drink.
Not my father.

Sometimes I wish he would.

MY FATHER'S LINES

In nice straight lines
He sets up pens
He orders life
He schedules plans

He sets up pens
The black, the blue
He schedules plans
For both of us

The black, the blue
Words on the fridge
For both of us
Tell where to go

Words on the fridge
Our whiteboard week
Tell where to go
The clock is king

Our whiteboard week
Filled to the brim
The clock is king
And I comply

Filled to the brim
A tight-run ship
And I comply
But it can sink

A tight-run ship
A neat abode
But it can sink
If there are holes

A neat abode
Is not enough
If there are holes
It fills up fast

It's not enough
He thinks that if
It fills up fast
He'll keep us both

He thinks that if
He orders life
He'll keep us both
In nice straight lines

ELIJAH LOOKS AT ME

as if to say, *Why*
are you back so soon?

I shrug. How can I tell
him I can't stand
to be around myself
for even five minutes?

Besides, I'm trying to
figure out who
this guy is.

This person
I called
Dad
but never really
understood.

THE OTHER PARENT

Why wouldn't you let me
live with Mom?
She would have understood.
She would have known what to do,
after that night, when everything
started spinning out of control.

Why did you insist
that I had to stay with you,
when it was so obvious
you didn't give a damn
and never had a clue?

She wanted to take me
when she left.
I screamed and cried.
Pleaded and begged.

You locked me in my room.
I didn't even get to say good-bye.
You said it was for my own good,
though you wouldn't tell me why.
But there was something more.
I could see it in your eyes.
Were you afraid to be alone?
Did you want to make a point?
Was it about control?
Or about being right?

BACK TO SCHOOL DAYS

"If you're done here,
then it's time for us
to go to the school,"
Elijah tells me.

"Why?"

"You have to go back where it happened
and make a different choice."

"No. I can never go up there again."

"Okay. Not right away.
But remember,
you don't have a lot of time."

"Never,"
I say, but then again,
I don't want to stay
here, either.

Because I can't stand
to be
in the hospital
for another minute
with my broken body,
with my token dad,

with my pain.

NEWTON'S APPLE

Elijah and I
get to school just after the
tardy bell rings. We

slip into Sci-Tech and then
hurry down the hall to our

physical science
class. Today Mr. M. is
dropping textbooks to

see if they fall faster than
feathers. Or maybe he's just

trying to make a
noise loud enough to get through
to the kids with i-

Pods. He gave up on sending
them to the office because

they got lost along
the way and usually
didn't come back. Now

he's dropping a book on the
desk of a girl who's asleep.

She jerks her head up
to look at him, turns off her
music, and says, "What?"

"What does Newton's apple mean
to you?" he asks. "Is it a

cookie filling?" she
answers. He groans and explains
gravity once more.

Drops another five textbooks.
Goes back to his desk and takes

a Valium. It must
get tedious having to
repeat everything

five times per class, six classes
per day, for year after year.

He must feel just like
a robot, but then, aren't we
robots too? Going

from class to class at the sound
of a bell doesn't really

make you feel like an
entity with free will. I
never considered

that the teachers were just as
trapped as we are. Maybe more.

Mr. M. has been
here for twenty-five long years.
I could make it out

in four. . . . That is, if I live
long enough to graduate.

THE BELL RINGS

Second period and it's time for
Elijah's history class in Humanities.
I freeze as we walk toward
the steps leading up to the
second-floor balcony, because
the H Hall is on the other side
of the glass window.
I can't see the Hangman,
but I know he's
looking down at me.

"How can you go in there day after day?" I ask.

"There's a lot of stuff in life
you just have to walk through.
Every time I walk through
that building, it reminds me
of where I don't want to go."

I look up on the second floor
and think about
the Hangman in the hallway.

I see
a baby pigeon
fall from the rafters
onto the ground below.
The two black birds are instantly on it,
like Brianna on a salad buffet.

I once wrote a poem
about a dead rapper
with a raven tattoo.

Ms. Lane talked
me into signing up
to perform it
at the school talent show.

She said I could be a great
writer if I stuck
with it long enough.

I told her what I really wanted
was to be an actress, and the real
reason I was taking her class
was so that I could write
better lines for myself.

She said that whether I became
an actress, a writer,
or both,
I needed to remember
that connecting with people
was more important
than outshining them.

But now I'm not sure
I'll get the chance
to do either one.

THE TARDY BELL RINGS

and we're still standing on the steps.
"I've got to get to class," says Elijah.
"If I miss another day, I'm gonna get ISS."

I look up at the second floor.
"I can't go in there."

"You can stay out on the quad."

"I don't want to be alone."

"Go talk to the Bird Man."

He points to a boy standing
on the circle in the center
of the quad. He's yelling
at the kids who pass.

"The seniors are gonna beat him up
if they see him stepping on the Raptor," I say.

"Not if they can't see him."

"What do you mean?"

"He's dead."

I shudder as I look at the boy wearing the school
gym uniform. I wouldn't be caught dead in that outfit,

and I certainly can't imagine spending eternity in it.
I'd rather do extra credit than dress up for PE for even a day.

"What happened to him?" I ask.

"Struck by lightning on the soccer field.
Go talk to him. He won't hurt you. His bark
is worse than his bite."

So I go out to the quad to talk to a dead guy,
because I can't stand the thought of going back
into the Humanities building. But all the time
I'm out there, I know there are eight eyes
watching me from the H Hall.

HELLO

As I approach the dead guy
I see him yelling at a group
of boys walking into the gym.

"That's right, keep moving, and stay away
from Ronnie if you know what's good for you."

"Hello," I say.

He turns around. "Are you talking to me?" he asks,
even though we're the only two people left on the quad.

"Is it okay if I hang here for a while?"

He strides across the circle until he's standing
nose to nose with me. "You're not dead."

"No," I say, and the fact that he realizes this
makes me feel strangely relieved.

"But you're not alive, either." He sizes me up.
"I guess you can't hurt anything. Come on in."
He moves aside so I can enter the circle. I step
on the tail feathers of the huge black bird and look around to
make sure there isn't a senior waiting
in the wings to beat me up.

"I don't get many visitors. Sorry the place is such
a mess." He tries to kick a Coke can off the circle,

but it doesn't budge. "Damn freshmen. Someone
needs to teach them some school respect."

"How long have you been here?" I ask him.

"Since 1985.
I used to stash my weed out on the far side of the track.
Was going to smoke some after PE,
before heading to the locker room,
but then a storm came up.
Have you ever been electrocuted?"

"No."

"I don't recommend it.
I was going to be
in the first class
to graduate from
Raven Valley High.

It happened a week before finals.
My grandparents were coming
all the way from Boise and had
already bought plane tickets.
They used them for the funeral."

A thin little kid carrying
a hall pass comes out onto the quad,
sees the Raptor, and decides to
walk across it while no one is looking.

The Bird Man runs to the edge
of the circle and screams,
"If you touch Ronnie,
I'm gonna rearrange your face."

The kid jumps back, like he's been hit,
and runs in fear in the opposite direction.
"Who's Ronnie?" I ask.

He points at the painted bird.
Then he points
at the sky where a black bird
is circling the school.
"That's Raptor Ron.
The official school mascot."

"He's bigger than the others.
I've never seen him before."

"Been dead for ten years.
Got old and
the hawks ate him."

"That's disgusting."

"That's high school.
Survival of the fittest."

GODS AND DEMONS

I wonder if the two black birds
who circle the school
are descendants
of Raptor Ron's.

Ms. Lane calls them
Hugin and Munin,
Observation and Memory,
after the two ravens who
belonged to Odin,
the Norse god
of death and poetry.

Their job was to travel the earth
and report what they saw.

"Exactly what a writer does,"
she told me.

I asked her if they represented
all memories,
or just the stuff
you'd rather forget.

She said mostly the latter,
but the birds weren't all bad.
When a group of settlers
got stuck in the valley
during one long winter,

ravens helped keep them alive
by bringing them dead pigeons to eat,
which is how the town
got its name.
And there once was a prophet
who was fed by ravens
while he was hiding
in the wilderness.

She said the prophet never died;
he just rode to heaven on
a flaming chariot.

But I can't imagine
ever being desperate
enough to eat anything
that came out
of those nasty black beaks.

And who wants to live forever, anyway?

I don't want to go back
to the hallway,
but I don't want to go back
to my old life either.
Maybe I could just stay
as I am right now,
hanging out with Elijah
and Oscar.
That wouldn't be so bad.

Is it a possibility?
Is there a door number three?

And if I open it, will I find
anyone waiting there
for me?

SPECIAL ED

Elijah comes back for me
for third period and we go
to special ed, where he's
a student aid in Oscar's class.

When Oscar sees me,
he starts pressing buttons
on his device that have been
programmed with redneck jokes.

They're stupid, but I still can't help
laughing, because he changes the
voice with each joke.

Elijah sets up a chessboard
and they play a game.

I like
how Elijah positions
Oscar's wheelchair so he
gets the view out the window.

I like
how unobtrusively he wipes
the spot of jam from Oscar's chin
that's left over from breakfast.

I like
how he talks casually, to pass the time,
like he's got all the patience in the world,
as he waits for Oscar to push the pieces
into place with his pencil.

I like
how proudly he says, "Oscar took
first place in the district meet last fall."

And I like
how when Oscar's machine says *Checkmate,*
Elijah gets a bigger grin than Oscar does.

ELIJAH'S ISLAND

The kids from special ed
get to go to lunch before
everyone else.

Elijah pushes Oscar outside
with his tray piled high with
pizza and fries. Then we sit
at a table on the quad, where
Elijah cuts everything into chunks
that Oscar can pick up with his fork.
Soon it will be too cold
to eat outside,
so everyone is relishing
the last few days of sunshine.

The bell rings and kids
pour out of the buildings like
mobs of ants scurrying from
their holes. They walk right by us
like we're not even there.
I know they can't see me,
but nobody acknowledges
Elijah or Oscar, either.

A few minutes later, they come
back out of the cafeteria carrying
burgers and salads and chocolate milks.
They sit all around us but never look
in our direction.

"We're our own little island,"
Elijah tells me,
"in a sea of wannabes,
princesses, and studs."

"Does it ever bother you?"
I ask. He shrugs. "I'd rather
have one or two friends I know
I can depend on than a crowd of
sharks just waiting for the
scent of blood."

I nod
because I know
popularity
isn't what it seems to be.

So why can't I picture
life without it?

They say people's greatest fear
is public speaking.

I've got that one down.

My greatest fear
is disappearing.

But isn't that
what will happen
if I go back to the hallway?

How long would it take
for folks to forget
I ever existed?

SURPRISE VISITOR

I'm surprised when someone sits
down next to Elijah, and I look up to see
my former best friend, Bri.

She shakes her head,
looks at the yellow tape
across the quad, and says,
"I miss Ally."

I miss Bri too, and that surprises me,
after what she did to me.

"She's not gone yet," Elijah tells her.

Brianna shakes her head.
"She'll never forgive me."

I get up and go stand where I can look her in the eye.
"Why should I forgive you? You ruined my life."

"I didn't send that picture of her and Davis,"
she tells Elijah.

"Yeah, right. It came from your number."

"I admit I took the picture,
but I never sent it to anybody.
Someone else must have done it."

"Who?" asks Elijah skeptically.

"Somebody who's at my house all the time.
Somebody who saw my cell lying around
and figured she'd get back
at both me and Ally.
The same person who sent the picture of her and Will.
I sure didn't take that one.
It's pretty sick to send it now,
after everything that's happened."

At the mention of Will, I feel my stomach
turning inside out.
Images flash across my memory.

Me with Will.
Darla with a camera.
"What picture of Will?" Elijah asks.

"It's been going around school all day.
I thought you'd seen it?"

Elijah opens his phone, and there's a picture
of me in the back of Will's pickup.
His pants are down around his ankles,
and he's lying on top of me.
Elijah looks up at me in
total disgust.

"I didn't send any pictures," Bri says.

But I don't care anymore
who sent the pictures.
What I can't stand is that look in
Elijah's eyes, because now he knows
I really am a whore.

Now there's no one left
to believe in me if I stay.

Or remember me
if I go.

ESCAPE

I run through the crowd
just trying to get lost.

Every time a camera clicks,
somebody dies.

I hear Elijah following, but
I don't dare turn around.
I can hear his footsteps,
but I can't bear the sound.

'Cause if he catches up to me,
he'll look me in the face.
And I'd rather disappear
without a whisper or a trace
than see the disappointment
in his eyes.

HIDE OUT

I dash behind the cafeteria
while Elijah gets stuck in the crowd
on the quad.

I see Will.
He's selling dime bags
to the same freshmen
he was beating up last week,
taking their money
with the same hands
he used to unhook my bra.

When we arrived at his pickup,
the night of homecoming,
he got a bottle out of the glove box.
Then we sat on blankets he'd spread
in the truck bed and started doing shots.

I knew better than to mix pills
with booze, but I didn't care, because
the pills had pretty much wiped out
any judgment I had left.

All I could think about was how awful
it felt to have Davis ignore me,
and how warm and wonderful it felt
to be drinking tequila by moonlight
with a varsity football player
who couldn't keep his hands off me,

who kept saying over and over again,
"I want you, Ally.

    I want you, Ally.

        I want you, Ally."

After a while
my body was burning and
the world was spinning
so fast I just needed something
to anchor me to the ground.

All I ever wanted was for
someone to want me.
Was that so much to ask?
So the next time Will said,
"I want you, Ally,"
I figured, what the hell,
and I whispered, "Okay."

All of a sudden I was flat
on my back with the full weight
of him on top of me, my spine banging
against the metal ridges of the
pickup bed, with the blankets
providing little buffer.

He pushed up my dress and
pulled down his pants so fast
that we were already doing it

before I had a chance to ask
about condoms.

He smelled like sour fruit,
and I tried to scream out the word
"Stop!" but his tongue was too far
down my throat for me to say anything.
All of a sudden I was blinking,
because a camera flash
was going off in my eyes.

When I looked up, I saw Darla
standing next to Davis.
"I told you," she said to him.

What? What had she told him,
I wanted to ask,
but I couldn't string together
enough coherent words to speak.

For a long moment Davis just stood there,
looking at me in disgust,
as Will continued to heave
against me.
He never even slowed down.

Then Davis turned and ran away.

And all I wanted
             was to disappear.

NOTHING MUCH CHANGED

for the first few days after that,
except that Davis turned away
whenever he saw me.

And that was before
any pictures had been texted.

Then one day at lunch,
when we were all sitting
together, Darla said
to Megan, "Where's Ally?"

"I'm right here," I said.

"I don't know," said Megan.
"I haven't seen her all day."

"Very funny, Megan," I said, poking
her in the ribs.
She didn't even flinch.

Why were they pretending
I wasn't there?

"Just as well," said Darla.
"I really don't like her
that much. What do you
see in her anyway?"

"To tell you the truth," said Megan,
"I don't really know."

Was I dreaming? Was this
some kind of psycho
nightmare? I had to
pinch myself to make sure
I was awake.

"You have to be careful
about your reputation," Darla
told her, "hanging around with a girl
like that."

I ran to the bathroom
and splashed water on my face,
then I looked in the mirror
to make sure I was really there.
What was happening?

Was I really losing all my friends,
or my mind,
or both?

THE GIRLS ON THE DANCE TEAM

started ignoring me
after that,
treating me like
I didn't exist.

Even Megan and the other freshmen
started whispering words
like *slut* and *whore*
when I passed.

Friday night Darla changed
the dance routine and
"forgot" to tell me,
making me look like
an idiot in front of the
whole school
during the game.

Afterward
I found
ten packages of condoms
in my gym locker
with a note that said,
"Hope these get you
through the night."

When Dad asked me why I was crying,
I told him I wanted to quit.

He said,
"There is no *I*
in 'TEAM.'"

Oh, Dad.
Don't you know?

There

is no

I

anywhere.

LATER THAT NIGHT

I went to stay with Brianna.
She was the only person
who was still talking to me.
Plus I was
hoping for a chance
to explain things to Davis.

I didn't love Will.
I didn't even like him.
What happened was a mistake.
A drug-induced nightmare.

While I waited for Davis to get home,
I tried time after time to start
a conversation with Bri.
But she just sat there
watching some stupid documentary
on whaling that she'd ordered from Netflix.

We finally went to bed around eleven
in silence.
At midnight I snuck into
Davis's room.
He wasn't there.

I went back at one

two

three

No Davis.

When I returned I found Brianna
sitting up in bed.

"You're not my friend," she said.
"And I don't want you coming over anymore.
The only reason you're here is because
you want to screw my brother."

Her words lay between us like a wall of glass.
Mostly because they were true.

WHEN I GOT TO WORLD HISTORY

the next Monday,
half the class giggled
and the other half looked away in disgust.
They were huddled around Megan.

My phone started to buzz.
I opened it to see the words
NEW PIX MESSAGE

It was from Brianna's
number.

I reluctantly pressed Open,
and a picture of me,
bare-chested, lying next to Davis,
flashed on the screen—
only you couldn't tell it was him
because at the last minute he had
covered his face with his arm.

My heart skipped a beat.
I wondered why
she was sending it then,
after all those weeks had passed.
Now I wonder
if she sent it at all.

"The Twins are looking healthy,"
said a boy in the back row,
and the whole class started laughing.

At that moment I wanted
to be invisible.

They all held up their cell phones
like they were at a rock
concert, and pictures of me
filled the room.

THE GETAWAY

"Where are you going?"
Mr. Jones asked
as I tried to run out of the room.

"The bathroom," I told him.

"Oh no, you don't.
You know the rules.
No passes for the first
ten minutes of class."

I cowered
in my seat
while voices
behind me giggled.

Sat watching
the clock until
the ten minutes
was up, and I swear,
time stopped.

And when it did,
a little voice
in my head
whispered,
You'd be better off dead.

GONE IN SIXTY SECONDS

In less than a minute
I was gone.
Whoever I was before
that moment disappeared.

Sometimes I can't even
recall who she was.

The girl who wanted to
light up the stage.
The girl who would stand
up in front of class
and make her classmates laugh
with her spoofs of Poe.

Sure, they were all laughing,
but they were calling me "ho."

I got a text from Cricket,
an old middle school friend.
I looked at my photo and cringed.
WTF. IS THIS REALLY YOU, ALLY?
DID U KNOW THERE'S A WEB POLL WITH THIS ON IT
CALLED PICK YOUR FAVORITE TWIN?

Cricket was going to a
high school ten miles away
in another town.

That's when I knew
there was no place to hide,
there never would be.

I was going down,
and there was
No. Way. Out.

BLOOD AND FEATHERS

Afterward

        pieces

                        of   me

        lay

              scattered

  across

                  the school

        like   the

            feathers

    of

                      a

        dying

      ˇ

          bird.

I RUN TO THE HOSPITAL

because I can't stand to be at school
and I don't know where else to go.

I lost Elijah on the quad,
or else he's decided I'm not
worth the trouble.
Either way, I'm relieved
when I don't see him following me.

As soon as I step into the waiting room,
I feel a crushing heaviness
pressing down on me.
I see my father sitting in silence.
His laptop is closed.
His pens put away.
His phone turned off.

"Ally, please don't go," he whispers.
"You're everything I've got."

Nana walks into the waiting room.
"Did you find Alice?"

He nods
and I experience such a sense of relief
that my heart could burst.
The weight of the room
lifts slightly,
and I feel that I can bear it,

bear anything,
as long as Mom is coming
back for me.

Dad has been looking for my mother.
That's what he's been doing all this time
when I thought he'd just been trying
to get in a few hours' work.

He finally gets it.
He understands
that I need to be
with my mother.

Thank you, Dad.
Thank you.

If I could go and live with Mom,
I could start over and forget
about the past few months.
I could clean the slate and
reinvent myself
in a brand-new place.

"When will she get here?" Nana asks.

"She's not coming," Dad replies,
and the room becomes as cold as ice.

"Did you tell her Ally might die?"

I hold my breath.
He nods his head.

And then he does something
I've never seen him do.

He cries.

"She made such a scene when she left," he says.
"And Ally has hated me ever since.
She never intended to take her, but she told her
to start packing. Why would she do that?"

Nana says,
"She was acting."

I FEEL MYSELF SLIPPING AWAY

First my hands,
then my arms,
then my feet.
Turning into mist
as thin as air.

I can't stay here one minute more.
There's not a single place for me.
Not at school.
Not at home.
Not in New York City.

There's only one place
where I belong.
I guess I've known that
all along.

The hallway.

ELIJAH RUSHES IN

and says,
"Don't go
back to that place."

Now it's my heart
vanishing into nothingness.
All the pain is gone
and the call
of the hallway
is inviting.

He says, "The pain won't last,
but death is *forever*.
Walk through the pain, Ally.
Don't turn away."

"You're wrong, Elijah.
Death is *never*
having to face
the truth."

The sooner I'm gone,
the sooner everybody can
move on.

And I feel the emptiness
in my mouth
and in my brain.

A FEW MINUTES LATER

I'm back
on the hall,
where I'm safe
and nothing hurts.
Where I'm not destined
to be a person with brain damage
or a disappointment to the people I love.

The Hangman is sitting on the tiled bench,
waiting patiently for my return.

"I warned you," he says.
"It's a cruel world out there."

"I know," I tell him.

"If you go back, the best that world
can offer you is a life like Oscar's."

He's making it up.
I'm pretty sure he can't tell the future.
And I could argue that I might
turn out like Elijah,
but is he really happy?
Is anyone?

"Besides," he continues,
"if you return to your
old life, it might be worse than before.
If you jumped off another building,
or put a gun to your head,
or slit your wrists,
you might not make it back here.
Let's face it, you didn't exactly
complete the job the first time.
This is a very special place.
A lot of people try to come here
but botch the job."

"Don't worry. I won't be
going out there again."

"That's good.
It's better for everyone that way."

THE HANGMAN'S ADVICE

Remember
when you
steal the pills,
turn on the gas,
sharpen the blade.

Consider
as you walk
that line,
you think that
you've
made up
your mind.

When you set
your pen
on the page
and tell the world
your last
good-bye.

Then place the gun
against your head
or take the plunge
or slip the knot.

Remember this
before you shoot
before you leap
before you drive.

You're gonna make
a mess of things
a wreck of things
you'll break some hearts.

You'll definitely
destroy some lives.

But there's no
guarantee

you will die.

PART TEN

T_ _ _ FAR
G_NE

Ally & Elijah

I REMEMBER

I remember
when I was six years old and my mother left my father
for the first time. She threw our clothes in a laundry basket,
put the foldout couch in a U-Haul trailer, and we drove
away, watching him standing alone in the driveway.

I remember
Mom telling me that as soon as she saved enough money,
she was quitting her job and we were moving to California.
She said I looked just like a little Scarlett Johansson,
and maybe when Mom got in the movies, I could
get in the movies too.

I remember
my mother had a hard time making it to work in the mornings
and we lost the electricity because she couldn't pay the bills.
We ate mac and cheese every night because it was cheap,
but she always seemed to have money for booze.

I remember
the night we got kicked out of our apartment and we went
back home to Dad because we didn't have anyplace else
to go. I remember the look of relief in my father's eyes
and the look of defeat in my mother's.

I remember
her saying she was sorry,
but she didn't sound sorry.

I remember
Dad saying it was okay,
but he didn't sound okay.

I don't remember
anyone mentioning
love.

The Hangman says
if I stay here
long enough,
I won't remember
anything   at   all.

I REMEMBER

I remember the night I almost died.
I went out to the old football field
looking down on the new stadium,
because it was the last place
I remembered being happy.

My brother, Frankie,
used to take me up there
to watch the football games so
we wouldn't have to pay
the admission fee.

Just him and me.

Drinking hot chocolate
and listening to the tunes
of The Fray
coming from the CD player
in his Camaro,
which he drove right up
onto the old field
so if we got cold,
we'd have a warm place to go.

Even when he started dating Pam,
he still reserved Friday nights for
football with his little bro.

Just him and me.

When I went up there
on the hill that night,
with the bottle of pills,
my boom box,
and Frankie's CD,

all I really wanted
was another chance to be
with him.

Just him and me

and eternity.
So I fell asleep to the tune of
"How to Save a Life."

But when I opened my eyes,

there was still only me.

AND A BOY OF SEVENTEEN

walking by wearing a rebel uniform.
He was barefoot and his head was bleeding.
"How did you get here?" he asked me.

"I took a bottle of pills."

"Then you need to go to the hallway."
He pointed at the Humanities Building
as his friends set up cannons
and sharpened their daggers.

I ran all the way to the quad and up the stairs,
hoping to find Frankie, but he wasn't there.

THE LETTER

Frank, I wasn't jealous when you said
you'd fallen for a girl whose name was Pam,
even though it complicated plans
we'd been making all our lives. You said
if you went to State, then you could live
at home and I wouldn't be alone
with Mom and Dad and nothing but the booze
to buffer all their unpredictable moods.

I'd watch Pam kiss you, watch how you would
stare into each other's eyes and then
she'd touch your skin like it was made of gold.
I never had a moment of envy

because I hoped there would come a day
when a girl I loved looked at me that way.

Please tell me, big bro, what am I to do,
give all my heart to love? What happens if
Ally laughs at me or calls me "freak"?
It's happened in the past. You know it's true.

Besides, I've seen the way she looks at him.
Davis Connor is the one she wants.
He treats her like a puppy on a leash,
but she just keeps on licking at his feet.

I heard the rumors going round the school.
I've seen the pictures, but I pressed delete.
I know she's been with Will, but I don't care.
Does that make me some kind of puppy too?

And if by some miracle, she loved me back,
could it work out, or would I end up like you?

DUMPED

When the next bell rings
I see Megan walk out onto the quad
and stand by the grass, expectant,
waiting for someone.

Darla Johnson comes out
of the gym and Megan
waves eagerly.
Darla turns and goes
in the other direction.

Megan won't take the hint
and hurries up behind her.
I see Darla mouth the words
Go away.

There's a look of
panic in Megan's eyes.
She's been kicked
out of the club and
she doesn't know why.
There's also the knowledge
that Darla could destroy
her. Darla seems to read
her mind, or maybe it's just
a general observation she's
making when she says,

You're not worth the trouble.

NOBODY

Megan sits on a bench
out on the quad and cries.
She's completely alone.
It serves her right.
I feel vindicated

for about two seconds.
Then I just feel bad for her.

For some reason I think about
the fact that she and Bri
were best friends
in second grade.
Then I remember
the tryouts for *Grease* in sixth.

Megan went out for the lead.
She'd never been in a single play
in her life, but she had the most beautiful
singing voice I'd ever heard. I was so afraid
she'd get the part of Sandy that I couldn't sleep for two day

But I came up with a solution.
One afternoon after drama class,
I was helping Ms. Smythe put away props
when I told her,
"You should give the lead to Megan."

Ms. Smythe looked at me in surprise.
"Why is that?"

"Because her mother is dying.
It might help cheer Megan up."

"I see," said Ms. Smythe, looking grave.
"But I'd hate to add to the pressure
she must be under."

The next day when the roles were posted,
I got the part of Sandy, and Megan got
the part of one of the Pink Ladies.

Megan's mother died a month later,
and she missed all the dress rehearsals.

I'd done the right thing by telling
Ms. Smythe about her mother. I really had.
But for all the wrong reasons.

GREASE

On opening night
I started crying uncontrollably
in the dressing room.
Brianna was the stage manager,
but she didn't know what to say
to console me.

I couldn't tell her what I'd done,
or she would hate me forever,
so I asked her to call my mother
out of the audience.

After Mom shut the door,
I confessed everything.
I knew she was the one person
who would understand.

She wrapped me in her arms
and I remember she smelled
like lilacs.

"You did that poor girl a favor,"
she told me.
"Now use that emotion.
Don't let it go to waste.
Get out there and sing your heart out.
Do it for Megan."

Mom always knew just what to say.
I instantly felt better,
and when I went out on the stage,
I gave the performance
of a lifetime.

As for Megan,
she barely remembered
her lines,
and she never tried out
for another school play.

I WONDER

what kind of girl
I really was.

The kind who would step
on her friends to get to the top.

The kind who would sleep
with a guy just because
she wanted to feel desired.

The kind
    no one will miss
        when she is gone.

AFTER THE SHOW

Mom took me out to dinner
at Le Chantilly to celebrate
with a bunch of her theater friends
who she had brought to the performance.

As we were eating our crab ravioli,
one of the guys put his arm around Mom
and said, "Ally was phenomenal. A chip
off the old block. Raw talent."

Everyone around the table agreed.
It felt good to have adults,
people who knew
what they were talking about,
admire me like that.

"Wouldn't it be ironic,"
he told Mom,
"if Ally made it to Broadway
before you did?"

The chatter around the table
fell silent,
the room grew still,
and the whole world
seemed to hold its breath.

At that moment
I saw something die
in my mother's eyes.

The man dropped his hand
from Mom's shoulder.
I could see he wanted
to take back his words,
but it was too late.

He hadn't meant to be cruel,
which made it worse,
because you can
disregard cruelty.

We all ate baked Alaska in silence,
and two weeks later
Mom packed her bags
for New York.

She promised she would
come back for me.
But she never did.

And now I know
she never will.

THE LOTUS EATER

"What do I need to do
if I want to stay here forever?"

"First, you have to forget."
The Hangman opens his hand
and there is a pale pink flower
sitting on his palm. Each petal
has a name written on it.

Megan, Darla, Bri, Davis

"Eat them
and the memories will vanish
like falling petals
blown away by the wind.
Eventually a few of them
will come back,
but by then it won't matter
because you won't feel
a thing
when they do."

I place Megan on my tongue
and let her dissolve.
She's bittersweet,
but when she is gone,
I don't feel guilty anymore.

Next is Darla,
acidic like aspirin,
but when I swallow
her I swallow my shame.

Bri nearly
gets stuck
in my throat.

Next is Davis,
sweet at first, but then
turning suddenly sour,
and when he's gone,
I'm surprised to find
that I don't miss him
at all.

A wonderful calmness
settles over me and I sit
down on the bench and smile.

AM I A FOOL

I won't lie
and say it didn't hurt
to see you with Will.

I won't claim
I didn't feel ashamed
for having such a stupid
crush on you.

I won't pretend
being your friend
doesn't leave my heart
black-and-blue.

But I will argue
in spite of it all,
for some crazy, stupid reason
I don't understand,
I still love you.

Is it too late?
Have you made your choice?
Is there anything I can do
or say
to make you want to stay?

THREE MORE LOTUS PETALS

Their names are
Mom,   Dad,   Elijah

I put Mom on my tongue
and she is gone before I know it.
Dad lingers longer than I expect.

As for Elijah, I try to take him in,
but can't get him past my lips,
so I fold him in my hand,
saving him for later.

Why didn't I call you
after that night
under the tree?
Things might have turned out
so differently.

I can still feel your arms
around me, and the softness
of your cheek
against mine.

I can't think about you
anymore, or I might want
to leave this place,
and it's all I have left.

Oh, Elijah, why couldn't
you have stayed
on the hallway?

Then I would have had
an eternity
to get to know you.

ALLY, DON'T GIVE UP

I go back to the school and walk across
the parking lot. I'm heading to the hall,
but when I reach the gate, I find it's locked.

I walk around until I see a wall
I can climb, and then I'm on the quad.
I take the stairs two at a time, 'cause all

I can think about is you. I've got
to try to reach you. Have to make you see
staying on the hall simply is not

all the Hangman says it will be.
He'll promise you a world that's free of pain,
but that's because a dead girl cannot feel

anything. You might not hurt again,
but you will never feel the summer breeze,
a snowflake, or an April-morning rain.

You'll never smell the forest, touch the sea.
You'll never get beyond the school, and you'll
wonder why the music has all ceased.

You'll never taste the kiss of someone who
loves you . . . the way that I do.

ONE LAST THING

"There's one last thing
you have to do,"
the Hangman tells me.

"What?" I ask.

"Follow through
with what you
tried to do last time."

"What do you mean?"

"You have to fall.
But don't worry.
I'm here to catch you."

JUST FALL AGAIN

The Hangman says I only have to fall again.
I'll drop into his arms and it will end.
All I have to do is take the plunge.
The girl in ICU will cease to exist.

I'll drop into his arms and it will end.
Nana can stop crying and move on.
The girl in ICU will cease to exist.
My father will go home and line up pens.

Nana can stop crying and move on.
I won't steal any more air from the world.
My father will go home and line up pens.
The line up on the screen will flatten out.

I won't steal any more air from the world.
It's time for me to end that life of pain.
The line up on the screen will flatten out.
I'll close my eyes and listen to his voice.

It's time for me to end that life of pain.
All I have to do is take the plunge.
I'll close my eyes and listen to his voice.
The Hangman says I only have to fall.

WHY?

So why

is it

that I

hesitate?

LISTEN

The door into Humanities is locked
and so I pound my fists against the glass.
I shout and scream. I plead and beg. I walk

the whole length of the building yelling at
the top of my lungs, just hoping you will hear
what I have to say. I'm praying

it's not too late. I know you fear
life is just too hard. Not worth the fight.
I have to go. Security is here.

But listen to this last word of advice.
The Hangman's solitude comes at a price.

FALLING

Each time I close my eyes it feels like I'm falling
into feathers scattered on a cloud of white.
But far away I hear a soft voice calling,

telling me that pain may seem consuming,
but *dead* is one long, dark, eternal night.
I close my eyes and picture myself falling

into the grave. There's danger in recalling
what it felt like when he held me on that night.
And now his voice keeps calling, calling, calling,

telling me to wake up and quit stalling.
It's time to make a stand and face my plight,
but each time I close my eyes it feels like I'm falling.

He says to fight the fear, but that's no small thing
when you're paralyzed and crippled by the slightest
thought of facing all the people who've been calling

you things anyone would find appalling.
And you know there's no way to make it right.
So I'll close my eyes and let myself keep falling
and I'll close my heart so I won't hear him calling.

NOT TONIGHT

But not tonight.

No need to rush.

For just a few
more hours,
I'd like
to keep
his petal
in my hand.

A LITTLE LIGHT

The sun comes up and I've wandered through
the city half the night thinking about
you, Ally, wondering what I can do.

Can I go to the hall and make it back out?
It nearly killed me last time, but I know
you'll die if I don't try. Another route

is what I want. What can I do to show
you, Ally, that hope is never lost? When it's
hardest to find, that's when you have to go

out looking for it. Just a little bit
will get you by. I've found it's just like light.
One tiny candle is enough to rid

the world of darkness, but you have to find
the flame, and I know that can be a trick.
Keep moving forward and don't look behind.

You have to keep on following the flicker.
Sometimes it's the hardest thing to do.
And here's the part that really is the kicker—

Your family can't always be there for you,
but if you have just one friend in the crowd,
that can be enough to see you through.

I must go in again. No path around.
It's the only way to get you out.

PART ELEVEN

FALL_NG

INT. HALLWAY—MORNING

I stand in front of the window and listen as the bell rings. Watch as the students all start scurrying to class like mice, trained to race through the maze, hoping for a little bit of Cheez Whiz at the end of the day. I've got news for you folks—there's no cheese at the end. There's just another pointless day ahead. You string these together and you call it a life, but it's not.

The Hangman stands behind me. He's watching them too.

HANGMAN
You're lucky you found your way to the hallway.

ALLY
I know.

HANGMAN
Are you ready?

ALLY
Yes.

SISTER
There's really no rush.

I ignore her.

HANGMAN
Remember what I told you. Just close your eyes.

I close my eyes.

HANGMAN

And fall.

I lean backward. I'm about to let it all go and drop into his arms when he says—

HANGMAN

And then you can stay here *forever.*

I stop myself. I don't know why. Something about the way his tone suddenly changed with that last word. It makes me recall what Elijah told me about pain being temporary and death lasting for eternity. Damn him for getting inside my head! I should have eaten that Elijah petal. It would have made this so much easier if I could forget him. I open my eyes and look at Julie Ann. She shakes her head in silent warning.

HANGMAN

Fall, I said!

I feel his rope slip around my neck and tighten. I gasp for air and start to panic.

ALLY

I can't breathe.

HANGMAN

You don't need to breathe. Just fall.

There is nothing reassuring about him now. I turn to look at him and see that his face has changed to a ghastly shade of crimson. A rope burn appears around his neck, raw where the skin has been rubbed away.

Rotceo strides toward me. His jacket flies open and I see that the shirt underneath is stained with blood.

ROTCEO
We can make you fall.

JULIE ANN
Don't, baby. Let her choose.

HANGMAN
The time for choosing has passed.

The red scar on the Hangman's neck turns black. As Rotceo gets closer, I see a gaping hole in his chest. Julie Ann tries to stop him. Her hair is on fire. While the Hangman pries her fingers off him, I feel someone tap me on the shoulder. It's the girl in black. She's soaking wet and her face is dark blue. She doesn't say a word. Just points at the doorway.

And there stands Elijah.

Wonderful, beautiful Elijah. Alive and whole and breathing like he's just run a mile through hell to get to me. Wet ringlets of hair cling to his forehead and his blue eyes are the color of forget-me-nots.

And that's when I recall . . .
a bracelet made of flowers

given to me on the night
of my first kiss.

And I remember
that I loved Elijah first.

ELIJAH
Ally!

My heart, or what used to be my heart, maybe it's just the memory of a heart, is beating so fast I feel like I'm going to explode. Elijah came back for me, even after everything he knows about me.

I pull the rope from my neck and try to go to him, but Rotceo blocks my way.

ROTCEO
You're not going anywhere.

ELIJAH
Leave her alone!

Elijah steps onto the hallway, and the Hangman is suddenly on top of him, pushing him to the floor.

HANGMAN
So you finally decided to come back and join our happy little family.

Elijah tries to get up, but the Hangman kicks him in the ribs, causing him to double over.

ELIJAH
(to me)

I don't have long. You have to make a run for it.

I try to break away, but Rotceo's grip is too strong.

HANGMAN

Ally's decided to stay.

ALLY

No, I changed my mind.

HANGMAN

It's a little late for that, but Elijah can always join you.

Elijah tries to get up, but the Hangman kicks him down again.

ELIJAH

Ally, this is the last time. I can't come back here again. You have to make a run for it.

HANGMAN
(to Elijah)

But why don't you want to come back? You know you want her. Look at her. Isn't she beautiful? Besides, everybody else has had her. Why shouldn't you have her too?

Elijah looks at me, and then looks away.

HANGMAN

She might not be so beautiful if she ends up like
Smith and Wesson. And what if she doesn't make
it? Are you going to spend the rest of your life
playing board games with Oscar? What kind of life
is that? You'd be better off dead. Even your
parents think so. They wouldn't miss you. Frankie
was the only one they ever cared about.

ELIJAH
(covering his ears)

Shut up!

HANGMAN

Oh, you worshipped him. Didn't you? But he didn't
even tell you he was checking out.

Elijah groans in pain.

ELIJAH

Ally! Hurry.

There is so much sadness and desperation on Elijah's face that I can't
bear it. I grab Rotceo by the shoulders and knee him in the groin. He
falters and I run past him, barreling into the Hangman with everything
I've got. Elijah stumbles to the door and opens it, and we both run out.

PART TWELVE

OBS_RVATIONS
OF TH_
NOT QUIT_
D_AD

Ally

WE RUN

down the G Hall
and through the front door,
going outside
to the second-floor balcony.
Elijah collapses on the
stairs leading down
to the quad
and starts to cry.

I sit beside him
and put my arm around him,
at least I try. He feels good and
solid and real, but there's
something between his skin
and mine. It takes me a minute
to remember I'm not really
here. "Don't think about what he
said. It's all lies," I tell him.

"Oh, Ally, haven't you figured it out?
It's all true. That's how he gets to you.
You want to know the real
truth about me?" Elijah asks.
"My parents can't stand me.
As for my brother, he didn't trust me enough
to talk to me about how shook up he was
after Pam died. He gave me his CD
collection. It was his last good-bye
and I didn't even know it.

Now I can't play a single song to even
remember him by, because every time I do,
I think I should have known what he was planning.
I should have done something."

He looks so lost that it scares me.

I think about how the Hangman called me
a whore and how maybe I am.
And maybe Elijah is right.
Nothing hurts quite like the truth.
On the other hand,
maybe I'm just a girl who liked a guy
and got screwed.
"You told me the pain wouldn't last, Elijah."

"I know."
He tries to take my hand in his,
but his fingers slip through mine,
and Oh, God!
How I wish I could
feel him.

"Come on," he says, standing up.
"There's some more truth
I want you to see,
and you haven't got
a lot of time."

CREATIVE WRITING CLASS

We walk in late and everyone
is working on the free write that will
consume the first ten minutes of class.

It's a different prompt every afternoon and I
wonder what today's subject is, because
every single person in the class
is writing furiously.

Elijah takes his seat.
Ms. Lane opens a notebook
and starts writing too.
I peek over her shoulder
to see if she's secretly
working on a trashy romance
novel she's planning to submit to
Harlequin, but what I see
is much more surprising.

She's writing a letter to me.

Dear Ally, please hang in there.
Come back to us. We want to hear
the rest of your story.

My breath catches in my throat,
or what used to be my throat.
Funny how I keep thinking in
body metaphors even when I
don't have a body.

I look around the room and realize
that they're all writing letters to me,
and my whole imaginary body begins to quiver.

LETTERS TO ALLY

I walk among my classmates and look
over their shoulders to read what they're writing.

Dear Ally, We miss you. Please come back.

Hang in there, Ally. This too shall pass.

You can fight this, Ally, and you can win.

*TEN PERCENT OF THE PEOPLE AT THIS SCHOOL MAKE
ALL THE TROUBLE AND THE OTHER NINETY PERCENT OF
US DON'T GIVE A RAT'S ASS WHAT THEY THINK.*
—from Corwin, the girl with the emo haircut
who draws manga figures in her writing journal.

*Ally, homegirl,
You can beat this rap.*
—from Dwayne, who looks very stoned
and seems to think I'm someplace
besides the hospital.

Dwayne walks up to Ms. Lane and points at something
hanging on the wall behind her desk, and I see
my poem. "We should have known," he tells her.

He takes my poem down from the wall
and starts to read it out loud.

"DEAD RAPPER RAP" by Ally Cassell

Once upon a Friday morning, almost all the class was snoring.
Our teacher left a vocab worksheet for a sub who was a bore.
While I nodded, nearly napping, suddenly there came a tapping,
followed by a man's voice rapping, rapping lines I'd heard before.
"I'm Skandalouz," the voice it muttered, rapping at the classroom door.
"Open up, or I'll kick in this door."

Ah, distinctly, I remember, it was a bleak day in September.
Dude told the sub he came to send her to a class on the second floor.
She grabbed her books and packed her bag, running past the man in black.
And then I saw it was 2Pac, standing at the classroom door.
"All Eyez on me," yelled the man, standing on the cold tile floor.
"I'm your new sub, Mr. Shakur.

"I'm here to wake you from your dreaming, give your simple lives some meaning."
He smiled at us, his white teeth gleaming, then he pointed at the door.
"If you're thinking about jetting, don't want to get caught here abetting
someone who'll have you forgetting what the h— this class is for.
If you get out now, I won't detain you, block you, trap you, or restrain your
exit." No one touched the door.

"Ah, I see you've all decided to listen to your uninvited
guest get down. I must confide that I've got a special treat in store.
Forgive me if my words are cryptic. Guess I'm just 2Pacalyptic.
Get off your butts, we're gonna kick it, like you've never kicked before."
And soon he had the whole class rapping and break-dancing on the floor.
Dancing on the classroom floor.

He rolled his sleeves and there I saw it, a tattoo of a black bird on his
arm, and then I heard the haunted whisper of the raven's words:
"Keep ya heads up, no regrets, don't know if heaven's got a ghetto,
but only God can judge what debt you'll have to pay forevermore.
He don't care if you scream and shout, 'cause big G knows there's no way out.
Once you've crossed the line—you're down, and you won't be getting up no more.
Hope you're open to suggestion, 'cause there only is one question
left. I'm pretty sure you've guessed it. Heard it many times before."
Ah, distinctly, I remember, it was a bleak day in September,
when I heard the raven whisper,
"What are you willing 2 die 4?"

THE LAST VERSE

When Dwayne says
that last line, he just stops—
dead. Then all my classmates
look at each other
in guilt.

It's just a poem, guys, don't
you remember the day I
stood up in front of the class
to recite it and you all
cheered for me?

It was in September. I'd just
hooked up with Davis and
my life was perfect.
I wasn't thinking
about dying.
I wasn't.

You're wrong. Don't look
at each other that way. Like
it should have been a sign.
I was happy then.
I was.

Okay, I admit I was a little
worried about having to keep
such a big secret.
I didn't have
anybody to talk to, but
I wasn't desperate.

I wasn't.
I really wasn't.

Was I?

WHEN WE LEAVE

I tell Elijah,
"I don't like the way
they were all standing around
feeling sorry for me."

"No, what you didn't like was
that they know the truth."

"Oh, and what is that?"

"That you're broken.
That you have been for a long time."

I feel indignation bubbling up inside of me.
"You're a fine one to talk.
You're a train wreck,"
I say, but then I feel bad,
because he's risked everything
for me,
and I've done nothing
for him.
Maybe I am broken.

But if he's insulted, he doesn't show it.
He just shrugs.

"We're all a little ruined, I guess."

Perhaps he's right.
"I just don't want pity."

"A lot of people care about you,
but they don't care about you because
they think you're some kind of superstar.
They care because they know deep
down inside, you're as
lost and confused as they are.
The problem is, you don't give a damn
what those people think.
You only care about the beautiful people.
Well, there they are." He points to where the girls
from the dance team are standing.
"Go ahead and check them out,
your former so-called friends.
See what they're saying now."

THE RAVENETTES

stand together talking
in the middle of the quad.

Darla walks up to them and says,
"Have you guys voted on
Ally's web poll?"

The other girls edge away from her.
"Are you serious?" says Lauren Payne.
"She's in a coma. Don't you think
you've done enough damage?"

"I'm just getting started," Darla replies.

My blood, or what used to be my blood,
boils inside of me. Oh, how I wish I was
in my body right now, because I'd use
my fist to knock that smirk
right off her face.

"I want to kill her," I tell Elijah when
I rejoin him by the gym.

"Good," he replies. "It was a turning point
for me when I wrote letters to my brother,
telling him I thought he was
a selfish bastard. Sometimes I still cry
for him, but I've given up the need
to throw away my dreams and die for him.

What are you willing to die for, Ally?
Are you willing to die for her?"

He points to Darla
and I shake my head.

"Then get on with your life."

"How?" I ask.

"You have to go back up there."
He points to the FAB.
"You have to remember
why you wanted to die
and you have to feel what it was
you weren't willing to feel before."

I shake my head.
"What if I can't?"

He looks at me
with his piercing blue eyes
and says,
"I know you can."

COULD I?

Could I really
go up there again?

Could I face my pain,
then click my
heels like Dorothy,
say, "There's no
place like home,"
and wake up
from this nightmare?

Could I
just slip back in
as quickly as I
slipped out?
What would it take?

Could I
close my eyes,
open them again, and find
myself back in the hospital room?
What if I never walk again
or talk again?

It would be a long road back.
So many things broken.
Elijah would help me.
And Oscar. And Nana.
And Dad.

Maybe Elijah is right.
Maybe just one or two
people are enough
to help you make it
through the darkness.

Could I

really believe that?

WHEN SCHOOL IS OUT

we go to Elijah's house
and he crashes on his bed
like he hasn't slept for days.

I crawl up next to him and try to gently press
my body against his so I can remember
what it feels like to breathe.

Breathe, I whisper to myself
as if this will resuscitate me,
but of course it can't be
that easy.

Then I sleep too, thinking
that maybe when I wake up,
I'll discover this whole thing was a nightmare.

But how far back would I have to go
to be able to wake up with a normal life?

Before homecoming?

Before the night I danced on the roof?

Before I ditched Brianna?

Before I kissed Davis?

Before Mom left?

And even if I did go back in time,
would I be smart enough
not to do the same things twice?

WHEN I WAKE UP

I see Elijah buttoning
a black dress shirt.

"Where are you going?"

"We—we're going to a play.
It's the final night of *My Fair Lady*."

"No way. You can't expect me
to go watch Darla prance around the stage."

"That's exactly what I expect."

"You've got to be kidding. Why?"

"Because she's who you could be in three years."

"The lead in the musical?"

Elijah shakes his head.
"No. The school's alpha bitch."
His words sting,
but his eyes are not unkind.
He's just stating a fact.

"You don't think much of me, do you?"

He glances in my direction.
"To be honest, I think you're one of the
most egocentric people I know.
But for some reason, I can't stop loving you."

THE FAIREST

I remember my mother's words
"Only one can be the fairest,"
and tonight it's Darla Johnson.

Her performance of the peasant flower seller
turned society darling is flawless.

But even though she's singing and dancing
with the other actors, she never really
looks them in the eyes, and you get the sense
they're really just props for her one-woman show.

For a moment I wonder
what life is like
for her at home.
What is it that drives her?
Does she have a mother
who left her like mine,
or a father who spends all his time
avoiding conversation?

At intermission I see
Brianna selling cookies.
Guess she decided
not to boycott
the performance after all.

When the show is over, the crowd has gone,
and the drama teacher thinks everything
is locked up tight, Darla and her friends go
up on the roof of the theater to celebrate.

"You gotta do this part alone,"
Elijah tells me. "If I go with you, they'll see me."

"You want me to go up there by myself?"
I look up at the place where I tried to end my life.

"You've got to remember
what happened, Ally.
Time is running out."

"What if I can't?"

"Then you go back
to the H Hall,
forever.
But that's not an option, okay?
I'll be waiting for you back at home."
He tries to touch my cheek
but only touches air.
"I'd wait for you forever."

THE LADDER

I look up at the roof, and
all of a sudden it begins
to come back to me.

I remember going up there
because I thought I'd find Davis.
He'd sent me a text:
ALLY—WE HAVE TO TALK.
MEET ME ON TOP OF BRADY.

I was so elated I snuck
out my window and ran
all the way to the school,
even though it was past midnight
and it was raining.

When I climbed up the ladder
and over the edge,
Davis wasn't there.
But somebody else
was waiting.
She was standing there alone,
in the moonlight, and
she was smiling.

It was Darla.

"Where's Davis?" I asked her,
and she shook her head.

"He's not coming."

The frustration of the past two weeks
caught up to me and I yelled,
"I'm the one he wants to be with!"

Her eyes narrowed into catlike slits.
"He wants to be with a lot of people.
I can't change that, but at least I can decide who
it's gonna be. I call it 'damage control.'"

"What are you talking about?"

"Did you really think I didn't know about you
and Davis? I set you up with him."

"Yeah, right."

"You want to know why I picked you?
Because desperate people are easy to manipulate."

"Whatever you want to believe."

"You think I'm lying?
I dressed you up and painted you up
and set you on display. Then I broke up
with him just long enough for the two of you
to hook up."

"You're crazy. You're just jealous
because you found out
he wanted to be with me.
He wanted to take me to homecoming,
and he wanted to meet me here tonight."

She held up something small and black,
and I cringed when I realized it was Davis's phone.
"No, *I* wanted to meet you here."
She deepened her voice, pretending to sound like Davis.
"Ally, you make me feel like such a man.
Ally, you're the one I really want.
Ally, I think about you every night."

I felt a cold panic seize me.
"You've been reading his texts."

She laughed out loud,
and her bellow sounded like the
caw of a deadly bird.
"Ally, I wrote those texts."

I suddenly felt as if I'd just discovered
the world was flat.
I shook my head violently.
"No. That's not possible."

"It wasn't that hard. All I had to do
was pick up his phone every now and then
when he left it on the table.
I loved your responses, by the way. So cute.
'Oh, Davis, your tongue tastes like a York Peppermint Pattie.'"

"Stop."

"'Oh, Davis, your hands are *sooo* strong.
I want feel them on my body *nooooow*.'"

"Please stop!"

"'Oh, Davis, you've made a woman out of me.'"

I put my hands over my ears and started to cry,
but I could still hear her voice.

"Yes, that's right, Ally. You were sending those texts to me.
By the way, that night when you were dancing on the roof,
I was the one who told Davis to take you home."

"Why?" I sobbed, humiliated to be crying like a baby in front of her.

"Oh, I think you'll understand in a couple of years,
when you're the one fighting to stay on top of the trash heap.
In fact, you may be one of the only people
who really will ever understand me."

I remember looking up at her
and wondering what the hell she was talking about.

"What did you say to him at homecoming?" I begged to know.
"You looked at Davis and said, 'I told you.'
What did you tell him?"

"Just that you'd been bragging about wanting to sleep
with every guy on the football team. Nasty double standard.
It's okay for boys to be whores but not cute little freshman girls.
Will didn't seem to mind, though.
I was the one who told him he should ask you to homecoming,
by the way.
I think you make a nice couple."

I leaned on the short wall that ran the length of the roof, because my legs
wouldn't hold me up any longer.
Then I doubled over because I felt like I might vomit.
The concrete below came into view.

Darla walked up behind me and said,
"There are queens and there are pawns,
and you'd do well to remember which one you are."
Then she left and I remember thinking
how easy it would be to fall.

WHAT I REALLY WANT

But I don't want to fall
anymore.

What I want now
is to walk through this shit
and get to the other side.

I also want
to know what's going on
up there on the roof.

So I push through my fear,
and I climb.

With each rung I feel
a stabbing pain
shooting through my heart,
but it's a pain I can endure
because I know it won't last.
And each rung I pass
makes me feel
a little stronger,
a little closer
to figuring it all out.

LIFE AT THE TOP

When I get to the top
this time,
I see Darla with her friends.
She's reenacting scenes from the play
with such frantic zeal I wonder if she's on crack.

I recognize something in her
the rest of her friends can't see.
It's desperation.

At one point they get tired of her act
and start talking among themselves.
That's when she jumps up on top of an air-conditioning
unit and starts singing "The Rain in Spain."

Is that what I look like,
a girl who has to be the center of attention
all the time?

Kids start making excuses for why they have to leave.

"Wait!" she says to Lauren Payne.
"I need you to help me run lines."

"For what? The play is over," Lauren says.

"For *The Glass Menagerie.* The community theater tryouts are
tomorrow."

Lauren just shakes her head. "I'm out of here."

As she walks toward the ladder, Darla grabs her arm.
"Don't you dare leave me. I can make your life a living hell."

Lauren shakes her off. "Yeah, you're good at that."

"I wouldn't be so glib if I were you.
Do you want to end up like Ally?"

I stiffen when I hear her
throwing around my name
as casually as she might
toss a heel of bread to a sparrow.
"It would be better than ending up like you,"
says Lauren, and I realize not everyone
has been fooled by Darla's act.
"I've had enough of your games
and so have a lot of other people.
I'm out of here."

Lauren starts to climb down the ladder.
Darla rushes to the edge.

"You'll be sorry if you leave me!"

"Oh yeah? Is that what you told Davis?"

For the first time
I realize Davis
isn't on the roof.

I didn't even look for him
at the play,
and I know I am
totally over him.

The pain in my heart
finally begins to fade,
to be replaced by a burning ache
in both legs,
a throb in my head,
and a strange beeping
in my ears
that sounds faintly
like the machines
in the ICU.
Could I finally be
on my way back?

Lauren leaves and Darla sits down on the roof,
banging her head against her knees and rocking.
The few people who are left
nod at each other
and slip away.

Suddenly Darla stops rocking,
frantically searches her pockets,
pulls out a vial, and
swallows a handful of pills.

Then she closes her eyes
and leans her head against the wall
as if she just drank a tall glass of warm milk.

Her face is different,
now that she thinks she's alone.
As if the mask she's been wearing suddenly slipped,
revealing someone scarred and sick beneath.

Or like when Toto pulled back the curtain
to reveal that the Wizard of Oz wasn't
some omnipotent being but really just a scared, little old man.

I smell rubbing alcohol
and see the glare of
hospital lights overhead.
"I am coming back,"
I say out loud.

From somewhere far away
I hear Nana's voice
as she tells the nurse,
"I think she's trying to talk."

"Nana?" I say,
and I can make out the trace
of her smile.

Darla's eyes snap open.
She glares at me and says,
"What the hell are you doing here?"

I glance around to see who she's looking at,
but I'm the only other person on the roof.
"Are you talking to me?"

"No, Sherlock, I'm talking to the pigeons."

"You can *hear* me too?"

"Do you think I'm blind and deaf?"

My heart starts racing.
Darla can see me.
I'm alive.

But wait.
This isn't the real me.

Darla closes her eyes again.
"Sometimes I get so tired.
Life can be exhausting."

Her hand goes limp and the
vial rolls out of her palm.
It stops at my feet and I take a look
at the label—oxycodone.

"How many of those did you take?"
Something is wrong. Terribly wrong.
I feel Nana and the hospital slipping away.
"Wait!" I scream,
but Nana is gone.

"Do you ever feel like the world is spinning in slow motion?"
Darla's words are slurred and labored.
She lies down on the roof and rests her head
against her hands in a makeshift pillow.

I rush over to her side.
"Sit up, Darla, you have to stay awake."

I don't know why I'm trying to help her.
I hate this girl. But I still can't bear the thought
of her overdosing up here on this roof.
What if nobody finds her? What if the ravens
started pecking at her eyes?
"Sit up!" I yell at her.
But she won't budge.
I try to grab her and force her up,
but that, of course, is pointless.

"You wanna know
something, Ally? I was always
a little jealous of you."

"What are you talking about?"

"People genuinely like you.
Nobody genuinely likes me.
I used to think it didn't matter,
as long as they respected me,
or feared me."

"Maybe if you gave them a chance," I say, but
she doesn't respond, and I see that her
whole body has gone limp.

"Somebody help her," I scream.
But the night is as silent as death.

Because nobody can hear me.
Nobody is coming,
and Darla
has stopped breathing.

I feel myself being pulled
back to the hallway again
as everything starts to dissolve.

First my hands,
then my arms,
then my feet.

No, I try to scream,
but my throat
has disappeared.

I fight against the feeling of desolation,
but it's too strong.
Despair keeps pulling
me
　down.

Even if it isn't mine,
it still keeps pulling
me
　down.

PART THIRTEEN

_ELLO
AGAIN

INT. HALLWAY—MORNING

I wake up to find the sun streaming through the plate-glass window of the hallway. They all stand in front of me—Rotceo and Julie Ann, the girl in black, and the Hangman. He points to the wall, where he's written the words:

<u>W</u>EL_OME <u>B</u>A_K

ALLY

You can't make me stay here.

HANGMAN

If you hate it so much, then why did you bring a friend?

He points to the far corner of the room and I see Darla sitting on the tiled bench, staring blankly out the window at the gate, where an ambulance is parked, and two men are placing a gurney inside.

ALLY

No!

I run over to her and try to shake her, but she's unmoved.

ALLY

Darla, why did you do it?

JULIE ANN
It'll be a day or two before she can hear you.
She's still assimilating.

ALLY
Come on, Darla. We have to get out of here.

SISTER
(touching my arm)
It's too late for her.

I sit down next to Darla, unable to bear the senselessness of it all.

ALLY
She wasn't trying to kill herself. She just took too
many pills.

The Hangman comes and stands in front of me.

HANGMAN
Maybe, but she's still dead. As for you, your time
is up.

I jump to my feet. It may be too late for Darla, but it's not too late for
me. I'm not afraid of the pain anymore. The only thing I fear is the
nothingness of this terrible hallway.

ALLY
You can't make me stay here.

He laughs and his voice echoes off the tile.

HANGMAN

Oh, and how are you going to leave?

I look at the steel door next to the bench where Darla is sitting.

ALLY

Someone will open it.

Rotceo gets up and stands in front of the door.

ALLY

Fine, I'll take the elevator.

HANGMAN
(blocking my path)

Everybody at this school hates you. You're a joke
to everyone.

ALLY

Not the people who matter.

HANGMAN

Smith and Wesson and the nut job, are you
kidding me?

I take a quick step around him, but he pops up in front of me, just as
quickly.

HANGMAN

Do you want a life like Oscar's?

ALLY

He's better off than you are.

I dart around him and go two more steps before he's in front of me again. I look at the elevator. This is going to be a tedious and painful journey, but I try to remember what Elijah told me. "The only way out is through."

HANGMAN

How is it going to feel when you see Davis making out with other girls?

ALLY

At least I'll feel something.

I make it halfway down the hall before he's in front of me again.

HANGMAN

And how is it going to *feel* when you look up at the hallway and know we're watching you? We'll always be watching you, Ally, for the rest of your life.

His words send a shiver down my spine, but I know I can't get stuck on this hallway for eternity with them, with their hopelessness and their despair and their watching. Always watching.

ALLY

Get out of my way.

I push past him, but he follows behind me, his voice just inches from my ear.

HANGMAN

You're a slut, Ally, and everyone knows it.
You wanted popularity and you were willing
to pay any price to get it. You're a cheater and
a liar. Do you really think Elijah is going to
forget that? Do you think Brianna and Megan
will forget that? Nobody's going to forget
that, Ally.

Just ten more feet to the elevator, but his words are like daggers, cutting
away pieces of me. I try to remember the letters the kids wrote to me in
creative writing class.

ALLY

This too shall pass.

HANGMAN

No, Ally. It won't. Because I know the truth about
your mother, about the real reason she left.

I feel like a knife is driving through my heart.

ALLY

She left because she wanted to be on Broadway.

HANGMAN

That's what she told you so you wouldn't feel bad,
but the truth is that you drove her away.

ALLY

No.

HANGMAN

You know it's true. You had to be better than
everybody, and that included her.

ALLY

She wanted me to be an actress.

HANGMAN

Yes, and she's the one who told you that only one
could be the fairest. What do you think happens to
the other one, Ally?

ALLY

I don't know.

Big, fat tears are rolling down my cheeks now and I can't stop them.

HANGMAN

She has to go away.

I cover my face with my hands. Is it true? Am I the reason my mother
left? It's too awful to consider.

ALLY

Leave me alone.

HANGMAN

Just say you'll stay, and I'll stop.

I put my fingers in my ears.

ALLY

I don't have to listen to this.

HANGMAN

Oh, but I'm afraid you do.

And then a cold terror seizes me, because I can hear his voice in my head. *Everybody hates you. It's all your fault. There's no way out.*

HANGMAN

Yes, that's right, Ally. I'm the voice in your head.
And even if you leave here, you'll never escape it.

It is his voice I've been hearing. It's the same voice that told me I was beautiful when Davis noticed me. The same voice that told me I was nothing when Davis dumped me. The voice that told me I was a slut and irrelevant and I had no friends.

It was the voice that told me I'd be better off dead.

HANGMAN

Ah, yes. Now you're beginning to understand.

ALLY

No!

But there are other voices, too. There's my father's voice telling me to wake up, the messages from my classmates telling me to hang on. There's Elijah's voice telling me to push through the pain. Even Bri, saying she misses me. I straighten up and look the Hangman in the eyes.

HANGMAN

So what are you going to do, Ally, when you're
back out there and the voice in your head starts
telling you what a terrible person you are? You
can't argue with the voice. That just makes it
louder.

ALLY

I'm going to tell it the same thing I'm going to tell
you right now.

HANGMAN

Oh, and what is that?

ALLY

Shut the hell up!

He tries to open his mouth, but it's as if his lips are sewn together. He
looks at me strangely then. Like he knows I've beaten him, but he's
not altogether disappointed. There's even a hint of a smile on his face
as he nods, then steps aside to let me pass. The other three join him,
and Little Sister gives me a thumbs-up. I walk through them toward
the exit. A thousand feelings bombard me . . . loss and loneliness.
Disappointment and despair. My head is throbbing and my legs are
aching, but I just keep walking. And when I get to the other side, I
realize the journey wasn't that long.

The elevator door opens, and there stands Oscar's special education
teacher, with Oscar beside her and Elijah next to him. She looks into
the hallway, then turns to Elijah.

TEACHER

I don't understand. You said someone was in
trouble.

I smile at Oscar and Elijah and they smile back at me. Then I step onto
the elevator and stand between them.

ELIJAH

Not anymore.

PART FOURTEEN

A FINAL NOTE

Ally

MY BODY

I've never quite felt like I fit into it.
When I suddenly sprouted breasts
and grew two inches over the span
of one summer, I felt like an alien
had invaded my body. When Darla
and her friends made me up into a
Ravenette, I knew it really wasn't me.

When I had sex with Davis and Will,
and they told me I was beautiful,
I kept thinking they were talking
to somebody else.

I was like a hermit crab carrying
a borrowed shell.

When I saw my picture on my cell phone
screen, it was the face of a stranger.

When I was a shapeless phantom following
Elijah around the school, I think that's the closest
I've ever gotten to finding out who I really am.

So when I look in the mirror at this broken,
shattered image of myself,
I just try to remember
this isn't me either.

And for my entire life
I've been an outsider in my own skin.

The real job will be
finding out who I am inside,
because that's all I've got left.

And for the first time
in my life,

that's enough.

WHAT I WON'T SAY

I won't say it's easy
going from class to class
in a wheelchair while people
in the halls whisper
behind my back, saying,
That's the girl
who jumped off the roof.

I won't say I don't feel
sick to my stomach
every time I see Davis
with another girl.

I won't say it isn't awkward
when Megan gives me a look
that says she wants to ask me
a hundred questions, but never will
talk to me long enough to ask a single one.

I won't say it doesn't hurt knowing
Brianna and I will never have
late-night brownie binges or
I may never dance again.
Or that my mother isn't
coming back for me.

But I will say
the sun is brighter,
the smell of fresh earth is sweeter,
and the smile of a true friend
is absolute heaven.

REWRITING MY STORY

Elijah pushes me to class,
places his hand on mine,
and God, I'm so happy I can feel
it, because it's warm and solid and real.

He bends down to whisper in my ear
and tell me, "It's going to be okay,"
and I love the way his curls tickle my face.

One day I will rewrite the story of my life,
and when I do, I'll start it with that night
with Elijah under the stars and that
first kiss.

Davis will get a chapter.

But Elijah will get
the rest of the story.

NOTE TO ERNEST

You were wrong.
Love isn't
something
you lose.
It's something
you find.

If you had
looked a little
closer
you would
have seen
it
everywhere.

PART FIFTEEN

AFT_R
WORDS

INT. HALLWAY—MORNING

The inhabitants of the hallway all stand at the glass, watching. In the distance they see Ally sitting in a wheelchair with both of her legs in casts. Elijah pushes her to class. He pauses and kisses her cheek as a light snow begins to fall. The inhabitants of the hallway all share a smile, except for Darla.

                    DARLA
          What is this place?

The Hangman puts his arm around her shoulders.

                    HANGMAN
          There are some rules you need to know, Darlin'.
          You don't mind if I call you Darlin', do you?

                    DARLA
          What are you talking about?

                    ROTCEO
          We have a special job.

                    DARLA
          What?

The Hangman points out the window.

HANGMAN

Make sure none of them end up where we are.
And if they do, and it's not too late, we try to piss
'em off so they'll go back where they came from.

DARLA

Why?

JULIE ANN

Because anger is better than despair.

DARLA
(stepping away from them)

Who are you people? What is this place?

Rotceo, the Hangman, Julie Ann, and the girl in black all look from
one to another like they're not altogether sure. Finally, the girl in black
shrugs.

SISTER

It's the hallway.

DARLA

I don't understand.

HANGMAN

Don't worry. You have an eternity to figure it out.

ACKNOWLEDGMENTS

Thanks to Stephany Borges, Dixie Colvin, and Pat Marsello for your willingness to tackle a verse novel and to my dear SCBWI friends, Lois Ruby and Kimberley Griffiths Little, for putting aside your ghost stories to take a look at mine.

This book would not have been possible without the generous support of my wonderful husband and children. You read multiple drafts of my book, introduced me to rap, and were willing to eat numerous frozen dinners from Trader Joe's. PS The 2Pac poster proved quite inspirational. And thanks to 2Pac for the song titles found in "Dead Rapper Rap."

Special appreciation goes to my amazing editor, Anica Rissi; publicist, Anna McKean; and the entire Simon Pulse team. I am so lucky to have you in my corner. Sara Crowe, I am fortunate to have an agent who helps get my stories into shape before the rest of the world sees them.

Lynne Ortiz, workout buddy, friend, and school social worker extraordinaire, you help keep me on track in so many ways. David Gonzalez, custodial foreman, thanks for the bird tales. I didn't know ravens ate pigeons and inhabited schools. Your anecdotes inspired some of the darker characters of this narrative.

Finally, to my parents. Thanks for naming me after the dead girl in "The Raven" and encouraging a lifelong love of Poe (and ominous black birds).

My gratitude to all of you,
Carolee Lenore Jochens Dean

ABOUT THE POEMS

Not everything is a poem.
Not everything should be.

Several sections of this novel are written in screenplay format. For me that is the best way to capture conversations between multiple characters. However, it should be noted that screenplays are never written in first person (Ally's point of view) as they are in this story.

Many of Ally's poems are written in free verse, but I did use several other forms such as the villanelle, because of its hypnotic, repetitive quality (see the poem entitled "Falling" on page 300). Pantoums are also repetitive, but to me they feel constricting since the beginning comes around again at the end. I used that form when I wanted to convey a sense of being stuck, like when you need to make an important decision, but the same thoughts keep circling back round again. "Just Fall Again" on page 297 is an example of a pantoum.

Other forms in Ally's voice include a cinquain chain, shape poems, a spoof of Poe's "The Raven," and several poems inspired by renga. Renga are strings of tanka inspired by an old Japanese party game. "Elijah Wears Black" on page 23 is an example.

When Elijah comes home from the psychiatric hospital, he spends an entire month speaking in iambic pentameter, a form popular with Shakespeare. Iambic pentameter has a rhythmic structure of duh-DUH / duh-DUH / duh-DUH / duh-DUH / duh-DUH. Many of Elijah's poems are written in iambic pentameter. My friend Caroline Starr Rose, teacher and verse novelist, likes to tell her students that iambic pentameter mirrors the beat of the heart. Perhaps that is why so many forms of poetry are based on this basic rhythm.

Blank verse is a form of iambic pentameter that doesn't rhyme. A sonnet is a fourteen-line poem, typically in iambic pentameter, with a rhyme scheme that usually ends in a couplet. This novel contains several random sonnets by Elijah—random because the rhyme schemes don't follow a standard pattern and often contain lines of blank verse. "The Curve" on page 173 is an example.

One form I used quite often for Elijah was terza rima, incorporating iambic pentameter in three-line stanzas with an interlocking rhyme scheme of *aba bcb cdc,* etc., and ending in a couplet. Elijah has six poems written in this form, including "My House" on page 171.

Dante Alighieri once created an entire verse novel in terza rima (though he used a slightly different meter). *The Divine Comedy,* written in the fourteenth century, is his most famous work. Some people think verse novels are a fairly new phenomenon. They are actually one of the oldest forms of literature. *Beowulf* was written by an unknown Anglo-Saxon poet using alliterative long lines somewhere between the eighth and eleventh centuries, and Homer created *The Iliad* and *The Odyssey* using dactylic hexameter around 850 BC.

What all verse novels have in common is that the poet first establishes a set of rules for the story. Sometimes these rules are quite loose and sometimes quite strict, but it is the poet who makes them.

And how often in life does a person get to do that?

For more details about the poems used in *Forget Me Not* and for ideas on how to create your own poems, visit caroleedean.com.